RAVENOUS GHOST MONSTER

GALLICHAN MANOR BOOK 2

KHLOE WREN

ISBN ebook: 978-1-922942-07-4
ISBN print: 978-1-922942-08-1

Cover Credits:
Digital Artist: Khloe Wren

Editing Credits:
Editor: Carolyn Depew of Write Right Edits

No AI was used to create this cover or story

To Katherine,
thank you for all the years of friendship and
support

CHAPTER

ONE

KATHERINE

Looking down at the certificate in my hand, my stomach churned. While I was proud of myself for completing the course and becoming a certified doula, I wasn't sure I wanted to follow the path that had been laid out for me anymore. I'd been assisting Rhonda, the current doula at Blackwell Retreat, with births for years, but she was getting older and wanted to retire. William Blackwell, the owner of the retreat where I'd been raised since I was a toddler, had offered me Rhonda's position, but I hadn't felt right taking it unless I was fully certified.

So here I was, formally qualified and expected to be back at Blackwell Retreat by the end of the week to start the rest of my life.

"Katherine? Oh, good, I caught you."

While the rest of my class had rushed out, no doubt running off to celebrate with friends and family, I was stuck here in the entryway trying to work out what I wanted for my future. Sophia's interruption of my introspection was a welcome distraction.

"What's up, Sophia? Did you need me to help you clean up or something?"

The older doula who ran the training center smiled gently and patted my shoulder as she came to stand next to me.

"You're such a doll. Always willing to help out. But no, nothing like that. We have a job which I think you'd be the perfect fit for."

That had me giving Sophia my full attention. I could always tell William that I needed to have some real-life training in the outside world before I returned home. Surely, he'd agree that the experience would be of benefit to everyone involved. It would also give me more time to decide if living at the retreat was what I really wanted for my life.

While William had created the retreat to give victims of domestic abuse a safe place to live, heal and raise their families, the children were more than welcome to continue to live there once they'd grown. Especially, if like me, we were willing to learn skills that were useful to the community. But living in town while completing this course had shown me how secluded things were at Blackwell Retreat. Listening to the other ladies in class speak of their families and social lives had me dreaming bigger than I ever had before.

"What's the request?"

"Well, it seems that Gallichan Manor has a lady in residence now. Lisa Gallichan has contacted us about hiring a doula for herself. She's four months pregnant, so the job will last roughly five months. Although, she did mention she was open to discussing someone staying on after the birth, if she was a good fit and wanted to."

I might have grown up secluded away from most things, but I'd heard more than one story about that place.

"Isn't the manor supposed to be haunted or something?"

Some of the stories were completely outrageous. Werewolves, ghosts and even one about the devil himself living there. I'd figured it was like what William had done with Blackwell Retreat. He'd allowed all sorts of rumors to spread to keep people away from those he cared about, whom he'd promised to protect.

Sophia waved her hand in the air. "Oh, don't you go believing those tales. An old place like that would no doubt have some drafts, and I'm sure that's what has spooked people over the years. Oliver and Henry caretake the place and have lived there for many years now, and they've never come to any harm.

"However, it's one of the reasons I'm asking you. Lisa's been searching for some time now. A couple of our doulas have gone out there for interviews but weren't a good fit. They weren't like you. With your upbringing, your feathers are harder to ruffle than most. What do you say? Take one job, earn some money before you head home?"

Sophia knew what my future held at the retreat maybe even better than me, and the older woman had not been subtle about her thoughts on the matter. One of the other things I'd learned living in town was that the townspeople didn't think much of those out at the Blackwell Retreat. Next time I spoke with William, I was going to suggest that maybe he shouldn't make the place so secretive. That while it helped keep the place isolated, it would hurt anyone who left to re-enter the world.

Frowning, I shook my head. "I don't have a car to get out there, and I don't think there's a bus that goes that far out of town."

"Oh, they have a driver, Henry, who'll come get you and drop you back home, including for the interview. You'll need to sign an NDA, but that's not unusual when dealing with the wealthy. What do you say?"

Having my own money would give me real options. With some cash to back me up, I had choices. While William would never force anyone to stay, there wasn't a way to earn enough money within the retreat to save to move out. Most work was done on a barter system that had everyone helping each other. Money that was made by selling to the outside world was pooled as a community and used to benefit everyone. Like paying for me to do my doula course. That was one of the reasons I'd never turn my back on the retreat completely. I appreciated everything William had done with setting up such a wonderful sanctuary and would always happily contribute to it. I just didn't think I could live there full-time for the rest of my life.

"Do you know how much the pay will be?"

"Lisa didn't tell me. She'll discuss that with you after you've signed the NDA, but she's getting desperate to find someone, and she wants to be the sole focus of the doula, so it'll be higher than standard rates."

I looked into her kind gray eyes and decided to be reckless and tempt fate. "There's no harm in doing the interview, I suppose."

A wide grin broke out over her face, "I was so hoping you'd say that. Come with me, and we'll go give Lisa a call."

COLE

As much as I understood why Noah and his mate, Lisa, wanted to hire a doula to oversee her pregnancy and birth, I hated that it brought strangers through the halls of our home. All my other siblings, aside from Noah, had fled the manor, but I didn't have the luxury of escaping. I envied my brothers, who could leave for long periods of time. The twins came and went regularly. Prior to mating, Noah would spend most of his time traveling to procure new books for his library. He would be gone for weeks at a time before returning with his latest find. Now he was mated, and they had a baby on the way, they'd decided to make the manor their permanent home. It was nice to have one of my brothers so close more often, even if it also meant I got to see them having sex more than I'd like. Noah was insatiable with his mate and he didn't seem to care where they were in the manor when he took her.

My cock twitched, but I ignored it. It was nothing more than simple envy for what my brother had. I didn't find his woman appealing in that way. Even when I'd held her beneath the water of my pond to keep her safe from her stalker, I'd not been tempted to sate my desires on her. She was a sister, my brother's world. But I couldn't help but fantasize what it would be like to have a woman of my own.

A feminine voice floated through the air to where I was lazing in my pond. Unlike the previous women who'd come, hers didn't grate against my nerves. No, her voice sent a shiver down my spine and had my cock throbbing. Maybe it was too long since I'd bothered to ghost into town to find a female to tease in her sleep, if just the sound of a woman's voice was enough to have me aroused. But no, if that were the case, I'd have reacted to the other women who'd come to interview with Lisa much differently. Whoever had spoken was unique, and I couldn't resist the urge to go find her.

Shifting from my slower monster physique to my much faster ghost form, I floated from the room and down the wide stone hallway toward Cole and Lisa's wing. Frowning, I tried to place the new sweet-smelling and somewhat fruity scent that hung in the air. It was familiar, something I'd smelled before. The closer I got to where Lisa was holding the interview, the stronger the scent became. The undertone of apple I could now taste at the back of my throat had me identifying it as a Ghost Orchid. I had several that grew in my pond room. They only flowered once a year for a very short time, and were the prettiest, most delicate flowers I had in my collection. Curious about what the female who would smell so good looked like and knowing she couldn't see me in this form, I floated into Noah and Lisa's opulent sitting room without another thought.

Unlike the newcomer, Lisa could see me, and she stumbled over her words for a moment when I rushed in, making me want to laugh. Since she'd completed the mating with Noah, she could now see us in our ghost forms, but the beauty sitting across from her couldn't see me.

Like always, being surrounded by such lavish trappings made my skin crawl. I'd gotten rid of much of the extravagant furnishings in my wing. Our father had decorated the entire manor as though we were royals, and this room was no different. There were oil paintings of long forgotten family members on the walls, and a thick rug on the floor whose intricate pattern complimented the drapes perfectly. Said drapes were currently opened wide, and the sunlight shone in, highlighting the freckles across the woman's nose and cheeks.

After loudly clearing her throat and raising an eyebrow in my direction, Lisa got back with chatting to the woman. I moved closer, inhaling deeply of the scent I could happily fill my lungs with for the rest of eternity. Even seated, it was obvious she was tall. Taller than even Noah's mate, who was nearly six feet. She sat straight, proudly and with confidence. Her long, thick reddish-orange hair hung loosely around her shoulders in waves and my cock twitched behind my tentacles as I wondered what color it would be once wet. Her full breasts pushed against the tight tank top she wore and with each breath she took, I found it harder to look away from them. Sliding further forward, I stood before her chair and reached a palm out to very gently cup one in my palm. She fit perfectly. I bit back a groan as her nipple hardened against my flesh and a shiver ran through her. When she rubbed her palms up and down her arms, I pulled away and moved to stand beside her chair, lowering my face close to her hair so I could breathe more of her scent in.

"For fuck's sake."

Lisa's words were muttered low, but my woman cocked her head in question at her as she dropped her arms down.

"Sorry, just felt a chill run over me."

Lisa waved off her words. "Oh, I wasn't talking to you. Sorry, this house has some, um, *drafts* that can feel like you're being touched. I'd been hoping it wouldn't happen during the interview, that's all."

A smile lit up my woman's face, and my breath caught. She was stunning, with naturally dark pink lips, and lots of light freckles over her skin that I wanted to touch and taste.

"That could get interesting. You have ghosts here? I mean there are all sorts of rumors, but I figured they were just made up by previous owners to keep strangers away."

Lisa winced and Noah, who was standing in his ghost form behind her, stroked his large palms over her shoulders.

"Yeah, that's gonna be something we'll talk about after you take the job, Katherine.

And something covered by the NDA you already signed."

Her name was Katherine. I liked how that sounded in my mind and couldn't wait to say it out loud.

Katherine laughed, and it was like a fire had been lit inside me. My chest warmed and my cock ached with need.

"If you hadn't already sold me on taking this job, that right there would have done it. I love to read, and mysteries are my favorite."

Lisa shook her head with a smile. "Well, you will certainly get that here." She frowned at me. "Perhaps more."

Katherine cocked her head again and looked in my direction for a moment. Oh, her eyes were the darkest of blues that sparkled with interest. It was like looking into the deepest part of my lake in the middle of the night.

"Right, well, can you start next week? Will that give you enough time to pack up your place and get things sorted to move in here? You'll have your own room, and there are plenty of spare rooms we can store your belongings in if you don't want to keep renting wherever you're currently staying."

When Katherine turned back to focus on Lisa, it was as though the sun had gone from the sky. I wanted her gaze back on me, even if she wasn't truly looking at me.

"I can be here Monday morning, but would you mind if I didn't move in straight away? Can we give it a month to see how it goes?"

Lisa nodded with a smile. "That works. I can understand being cautious. Do you have a car? Henry will be happy to drive you back and forth if you don't."

Lisa might be okay with that, but I wasn't. Katherine was mine. I felt it down to my soul. I needed to have her under the manor's roof so I could protect her, knowing she was safe. Unlike my siblings, I couldn't leave the manor to follow her around until she returned. I could only leave for several hours at the most, and if I left for that long, I'd be very weak afterward and need to recuperate out in the lake. I hated having to do that, but she was worth it.

After taking another long look at Katherine, I turned to Noah and nodded to the door. He pressed a kiss to his mate's head before he followed me out.

"Brother, Katherine is not here for you."

I raised a brow at Noah. "Like Lisa was only here for your library?"

He went to respond but I shook my head. "No. Katherine is mine as Lisa is yours. I will keep her guarded. I will go home with her when she leaves, and make sure her home is safe."

Noah frowned. "She lives on the other side of Batsonville, a twenty-minute drive. That's too far for you to ghost there yourself. It won't be easy for you to return to your pond each day."

"I'll discuss with Henry him driving me in and out until she starts work, then I'll simply travel with him when he takes her back and forth from the manor."

Henry was our butler and driver. Like Oliver, our cook, he was human but knew all about those who called this manor home. He was not afraid when ghosts spoke with him.

It was currently Monday, so it would be a full week before Katherine would begin to spend her days here. I wished I could spend the entire time with her, but I couldn't be away from my pond or the manor's lake for that long.

Thanks to our father, all my siblings and I were cursed. We were each now monsters, with a ghost form and a visible one. We each had horns and fangs, but I was the only one with tentacles instead of legs. The only one who was tied to the water here at the manor. It was frustrating to be limited in such a manner, but I wouldn't let anything stop me from courting Katherine. I would spend the nights in my ghost form, entering into Katherine's dreams, making her mine so when next Monday came around, she'd be familiar with me and hopefully accepting of my monster form. I am very skilled with my tentacles. She will be well pleasured and fully sated every day. Hopefully, I can convince her to move to the manor sooner.

The sensitive tips of my tentacles buzzed and twitched with my eagerness.

"When Katherine moves in, she'll be in the room beside my pond. I want her close."

Noah shook his head. "She should be close to Lisa and the baby. She should be in our wing."

"So she can listen to you two fucking all night and day? I think not. My rooms are not so far from yours. She will be moved into my wing."

Noah rubbed a hand over his face. He was the eldest of us and often tried to take on a fatherly role. Normally, I was happy to follow his lead, but not this time. Not when it came to Katherine.

"Fine, brother. She will live in your wing. But if she's not accepting of your attentions, you are not to force her. We need her for Lisa. None of the others have been suitable. After weeks of interviews, Katherine is the first one Lisa has connected with, and she seems unafraid of ghosts. I will not allow you to scare her away."

I scoffed, waving off my brother's concerns, confident that fate had sent Katherine to be my mate. "She will not run from me but rather to me."

"If you are going to chase after her, make yourself useful and investigate for any threats that could follow her here."

I nodded. Lisa had a stalker who'd come to the manor and put her life at risk. I wouldn't allow something like that to happen to my woman if I could help it.

"I will make sure she is safe."

Noah grunted before he turned and went back into the sitting room to join the women. I didn't follow but returned to my pond. I needed to soak for as long as possible before I left with Katherine so I could extend my time away from the manor.

CHAPTER
TWO

KATHERINE

Settling into the limo to be driven back home after my interview, I had to smile. Gallichan Manor was going to be so much fun to explore. Lisa was four months pregnant and healthy. She'd implied the baby may not be normal, but when I'd tried to get her to explain what she meant, she gave me a serene smile and told me she'd clarify after I'd taken up residence. Naturally, I'd accepted the position, but couldn't bring myself to agree to move in just yet. I needed to get to know Lisa better, work out what exactly was going on in the manor before I did. I was also a little in shock at the obscene amount of money they were offering. Even if I didn't stay past the birth, I'd have more than enough saved to have real options at the end.

Blackwell Retreat would always be home, and I'd continue to return to visit my mom and the others, but I could be their doula without living there. The more time I spent away from the safety of its confines, the clearer it became. I wanted more out of life than what the retreat could offer.

Absently, I rubbed my hand over my right boob, my flesh still tingling from whatever had happened back at the manor. It felt like someone had palmed me, giving my breast a slight squeeze, which had me grinning. The stories of Gallichan Manor being haunted may be more than rumors after all. Not only did I enjoy reading mysteries, but I was also completely addicted to ghost hunting videos on YouTube on my phone. Much to my devout Christian mother's frustration, the supernatural had always interested me. Living a normal, standard life was way too boring for my tastes. Which probably explained my restlessness about the thought of living the rest of my life within the confines of Blackwell Retreat.

With a sigh, I closed my eyes and wriggled in against the soft leather seat to have a nap on my way home. It was damn nice having someone drive me around instead of waiting on buses. I could definitely get used to this part of the job.

In the space of one day, I'd gone from worrying about how I was going to cope returning home and being stuck there after experiencing the outside world, to having a job that paid so well that once it was done, I'd be able to take some time to work out where I wanted to settle and establish my life.

The car pulling to a stop had me jerking me out of my thoughts and with a shake of my head, I grabbed my bag. Before I could open the door, Henry was there doing it for me.

"Thanks, Henry."

"You're most welcome, Miss Turner. I look forward to seeing you soon."

With a smile, I waved before turning to walk toward my apartment building. Once through the door, I nearly ran up the stairs and down the hallway with all the excitement I had running through my veins. Once inside, I looked around the living area of my one-bedroom apartment. I'd told Lisa I needed a month, but I doubted I'd last that long. This place was a dump and even if it wasn't, I doubted anything could compare to the manor house. I hadn't seen a bedroom, but I could imagine how luxurious they would be.

Maybe I should have agreed to move straight in, but that seemed like a dangerous thing to agree to so quickly. I needed to play it cool, not act like I was raised in a commune by an overprotective mother and a bunch of other people who were equally paranoid about the outside world. William had done a fabulous job setting up the retreat for anyone who'd suffered abuse. Many women came there pregnant or with young children with nothing but the clothes on their backs. They were always welcome, and a home was made for them. But they understandably didn't want to leave to give birth.

Guilt ate at me again for even thinking about not going back. But I didn't need those high fences to make me feel safe. As I'd grown older, they'd felt more suffocating than secure. A vision of Ash's smirking face had a shudder running through me. Sometimes, it seemed like genetics were stronger than upbringing. Ash's father was a bastard who'd beaten his mother to the point she had a miscarriage. His mom was the sweetest woman, but Ash was more like his father, possessive with a mean streak. He'd not been subtle in letting me know he considered me his. Just like I'd been equally clear in letting him know no man would ever own me. I'd made the mistake of sleeping with him once, but I had no intention of repeating that mistake. Thankfully, he knew if he forced himself on me, he would get kicked out of the retreat. William had a zero-tolerance policy on that type of behavior.

Needing to clear my mind, I went to my bedroom and stripped out of my clothes, tossing them into my laundry basket. In nothing but panties, I pulled out my dresser drawers for my workout clothes. Pulling on my sports bra, I had my arms stretched up and the fabric over my face when tingles spread over both my breasts, just like back at the manor. With a gasp, I pulled the bra back off and tossed it aside before looking in the mirror. Something was definitely touching me, cupping my boobs and lifting them. It was damn surreal to see the girls moving without anything touching them.

Ghosts, indeed.

"Guess you followed me from Gallichan Manor, huh?"

Warmth engulfed the tip of my right breast, and a shiver ran down my spine when the other nipple was pinched and twisted.

"Ghost with a boob fetish. My lucky day."

Heat pooled low in my belly as the ghost continued to work my breasts with its mouth and fingers. My gaze stayed glued to the mirror, on how red my nipples were getting, I started to rub my thighs together.

"So, ghostie, you a boy or a girl?"

I was honestly horny enough I didn't really care, but damn, I was hoping it was a male ghost because I could use a dick right about now. I'd always had a high libido, but mostly dealt with it myself. It wasn't like there was a heap of options at the retreat, and those options were often like Ash, thinking he owned a girl if she opened her legs to him. But I'd watched enough TV to know that wasn't how the rest of the world worked. It might be nice to give my dildo a break for one night.

"My name is Cole, not ghostie."

His deep voice rumbled over my nerves.

"Boy ghost then. Good."

Something warm and slick covered the tip of each breast a moment before a gentle suction tugged on both my nipples. With a gasp, I threw out an arm to press my hand against the wall. I had no fucking idea how he'd managed to do what he was doing, but I never wanted him to stop.

"You are not afraid that I'm a ghost?"

I shook my head. "Ghosts fascinate me. Never actually met one before, and didn't realize they could..." My voice trailed off as my panties started to slide over my hips and down my legs until they dropped to the floor around my feet.

"Put your back against the wall, then spread your legs."

His voice was low, so compelling, that almost before I could process the request, I was moving, pressing my spine against the smooth wall as I lifted each foot out of my underwear before moving them to shoulder width apart.

The cool air of the room rushed over my wet folds, sending a shudder through me as I pressed my palms against the wall. It was strange to not be able to see or reach out and touch someone I knew was in front of me. A startled shriek left me when something smooth and slick slithered around my waist, gripping me before lifting me. Then two more appendages wrapped around each of my ankles and spread my legs further apart. Before I could question what he was doing, heat engulfed my bare mound. He nibbled at my folds before he slid his tongue within me and I arched my back, pressing my breasts tighter to whatever was suctioning against them as waves of arousal shot through me. When another of the suctiony things attached to my clit, my vision blacked out for a moment at the insane amount of pleasure he was giving me.

Tilting my hips, I began to thrust against Cole's tongue as my climax barreled closer. His low growl was the only warning I got before something blunt but thinner than a cock pressed against my back entrance. It teased and rimmed me until the muscles loosened and allowed him to slip inside. Then he was fucking my ass while he continued to make a meal out of my pussy. My mind was overwhelmed, unsure of what to focus on. My boobs were overly sensitive, and my clit was burning while my channel clenched against the thick, warm tongue that continued to fuck me while the nerves in my ass lit up at the stimulation of what had to be some sort of tentacle that was stroking in and out of me.

With a whimper, I fell over the edge into bliss, coming harder than I ever had before. My vision turned black while all I could hear was ringing in my ears and my entire body was a live wire.

COLE

As my woman continued to tremble after her climax, I moved her over to the bed, laying her out on the covers. My cock was hard and throbbing with the need to mark her as mine. To fill her belly, her womb and her ass, then cover her skin in my cum. The urge was deep, an animalistic instinct I struggled to resist to act on immediately.

I still had a tentacle deep in her ass and I continued to slowly pump it in and out of her. Then I slipped another into her pussy, searching for that little spot I knew would send her higher. Once I had her G-spot located, I set one of my suction cups over it and began to pulse against it. Her body jerked as another sexy whimper left her lips. Moving up the bed toward her head, I was careful to keep my tentacles where they were, pleasuring my mate well.

"Open your mouth for your mate's cock."

In my ghost form, my voice was irresistible to humans. She had to comply with whatever order I issued. And she did so now, licking her plump, red lips before opening them wide. Holding my cock, I ran the tip over her lips before slipping between them and entering the wet warmth of her mouth.

"Lick and suck me until I fill your belly."

With a groan, she twirled her tongue around the head of my dick then sucked me in until I was touching the back of her throat, which had me moaning. So good. She felt so fucking good. Unlike my brothers, I hadn't had many lovers. Since I'd only ever been able to leave the grounds for short periods of time, a woman would need to be local for me to visit her, and not many of those had ever interested me. And no one had ever caught my attention like Katherine. She was perfection, and I couldn't wait to claim every part of her.

Unable to hold off any longer, I started to thrust my hips, fucking her mouth with deep thrusts that filled her throat. In my ghost shape, I could allow her to feel me as though I were a normal man while allowing air to pass through me so she could breathe normally. That meant I could stay in her throat for longer on each stroke than I could if I were in my monster form.

It was only a matter of minutes before I erupted, coming straight down her throat and filling her belly with my seed. I pulled out in time for the last few spurts to land over her lips and chin.

"Close your eyes, *la sirena.*"

Her lids lowered, and I lifted a palm, spreading my cum over her face and neck.

The shimmer it left on her skin had my cock hardening again. I'd never had the urge to do this to another woman, so I had no clue how long the shimmer would last. I hoped it didn't wash off easily, although, if it did, I'd happily renew my mark on her.

When I was done, she squirmed against the sheets while she licked her lips with a moan. I lowered down and covered her mouth with mine, kissing her deeply as I curled tentacles around each of her breasts to squeeze as the tips teased her nipples.

"More, Cole. I need more."

With a grin, I lifted away from her and looked down her body, her pussy bare and glistening. Gripping my cock in my palm, I lined the head up with her entrance, rubbing the head in her cream. I was huge against her smaller form, but I knew she could take me. Deep in my soul, I knew she was made for me. Fitting a suction cup over her clit again, I pulsed against the hard little nub as I began to press into her for the first time.

Her back arched and she threw her hands out, taking fistfuls of bedding as she stretched to accommodate my thick cock. My gaze ate up the sight she made, writhing for me. When I came up against her cervix, there was still an inch or so of me left outside her body. I didn't want to hurt my woman, but I needed to be rough. Wrapping a palm around the base of my dick to make sure I wouldn't go too deep and hurt her, I pulled out and slammed back in. Her channel rippled around me when I thrust home again, and on the third stroke, she planted her feet on the mattress and tilted her hips up against me each time I filled her.

My fangs dropped as my arousal spiraled higher. Every suction cup tingled with pleasure, and my balls drew up, ready to fill my mate's womb. With one last thrust in, I stayed deep inside her as my cock jerked with each jet of my seed. I teased her clit and nipples as I emptied myself, not stopping until she clenched around me with her own orgasm.

THREE

KATHERINE

STILL HALF ASLEEP, I stumbled into the bathroom but froze when I caught sight of my arm in the morning light as I reached to turn on the shower.

"What the hell?"

I tilted my arm back and forth to take in the shimmer before I looked down. My entire body sparkled. I rubbed at my tummy, but it didn't budge. Quickly adjusting the water, I jumped in under the spray and grabbing my loofah, soaped it up and started scrubbing.

"Cole, if you're still here, you need to start explaining this shit right now."

Silence greeted me. Great. Bastard had

abandoned me now that he'd had his fun. After scrubbing and rinsing my legs, I sighed with relief that the shimmer was gone. At least it wasn't permanent. As I continued to wash the rest of my body, I vaguely recalled Cole rubbing his cum into my skin several times during the night.

"Bastard marked me, then up and left this morning without even a goodbye."

If I hadn't already accepted the job at the manor, I would have now just so I could go track Cole's butt down and rip him a new one. This was not cool. Not at all. I didn't want to walk around every day looking ready for my turn dancing around a pole.

Once I was clean, dried and dressed, I sat on my couch and stared at my phone. I should call home to let Mom and William know my change of plans, but I wasn't sure what I'd tell them if they asked when I was going to come back. They weren't expecting me to return until the end of the week, so I had a little time to plan what I'd tell them.

I jerked when my phone rang in my hands, then winced when I saw the number. Speaking of things I wouldn't miss about the retreat...

"Hi, Ash. What's up?"

"Hey, Katherine. Just wondering what time you want me to come pick you up and bring you back home?"

I pinched the bridge of my nose. "I'm not due back until the end of the week, Ash."

"Yeah, but you finished your course. There's no reason for you to stay away from where you belong any longer."

"No one needs a doula right now, and if they did, Rhonda can handle it. I've got an interview today for a job here in town."

He didn't need to know I'd already had the interview and accepted the job.

His growl sent a shiver through me, but not in a good way.

"You don't need to look for a job, you have one here. You need to come home, girl."

My temper flared brightly. "I'm not a girl, I'm a damn adult and I can make my own decisions. I'm checking out this job whether you like it or not. You are not the boss of me, Ash. You never were, and you never will be."

I hung up before he could respond, but fury now coursed through my veins. How dare he? Had he learned nothing from how we were raised and from the stories the women and men had shared about their lives prior to coming to Blackwell Retreat.

I'd lied about going to the interview, but maybe I could go back out to the manor and chat with Lisa some more. Maybe she'd let me explore the house and grounds. While I was there, I could hopefully track down Cole and have some words. It was so not okay to mark me, keep me up half the night, then vanish on me in the morning. He'd touched me up at the manor while it had been daytime, so it wasn't that he could only come out at night.

My anger fled as arousal took its place now that I was remembering last night. I clenched my thighs as heat pooled in my pussy. Hopefully, he'd apologize with his tongue or cock. Damn, but he had a spectacular dick. There was an ache deep inside from how well he'd fucked me. It was a nice ache, one I'd happily enjoy every day. Damn, but I loved sex. Always had. There weren't many options for partners at the retreat, and I sure as hell wasn't letting Ash touch me again. I'd mostly relied on toys to take the sexual edge off, but they had nothing on Cole. Being a ghost, I wasn't sure what he looked like, but he had to have tentacles in order to do what he'd done to me. I was extremely curious about how he looked, what color his skin was, how many tentacles he had... but I guess that would remain a mystery since I couldn't actually see him.

A new thought flashed through my mind that left my blood running cold.

He'd not only covered me in his cum, but he'd also left his seed inside me too. I was on birth control, so I wasn't worried he'd knocked me up, but I couldn't help but wonder if Cole was the father of Lisa's baby?

"No way."

I would not be the other woman. If Cole was Lisa's baby daddy, I would turn down the job and go back to the retreat.

Needing to know if I was worrying about nothing, I grabbed my phone and called Lisa.

"Hi, Katherine, is everything all right?"

"Oh, yes, everything's fine. I just thought of a few more questions but wanted to chat to you in person. Can I come out now?"

"Of course! Want me to send Henry to come get you?"

Traveling regularly in a limo with a

driver was going to take some getting used to. "Don't bother him about it. I'll just Uber it out there."

"If you're sure."

"Yep, totally sure. I'll see you soon."

"See you then."

After ending the call, I pulled up the app and ordered an Uber. Thankfully, there was one close, and I rushed to grab my bag and get out of the building in time to meet it.

By the time my ride pulled up in front of the row of white columns that dominated the manor's facade, I was starting to rethink my plan. What if Cole wasn't even here? Would Lisa think I was crazy and pull the job offer? Before I could tell the driver to take me back to my apartment, Lisa came through the huge front doors, a frown on her face as she came closer. With a false smile, I thanked the guy driving me, then got out. He wasted no time in taking off. The entire drive out he'd told me I was mad for coming anywhere near this place.

I probably shouldn't risk this job by asking Lisa outright who her baby's daddy was, but I couldn't really question Cole about it. It would be too easy for him to lie to me, and with him being a damn ghost, I couldn't exactly read his body language.

"Hi, Katherine. Why don't you come on in and we'll have a drink. You a coffee or tea drinker?"

A shudder ran through me. "No coffee, but I do love a nice cup of tea. Especially if you have flavored ones. The more obscure, the better."

Lisa laughed. "You're gonna fit in around here just fine. We have quite the selection."

KATHERINE

Lisa's calmness was contagious, and by the time I followed her into the kitchen, I was wondering if I hadn't blown everything out of proportion by overthinking it all. Although, it was hard not to obsess over a night spent being fucked by a ghost. After he'd worn me out and I'd fallen asleep, I'd had several extremely vivid dreams that starred my favorite ghost, and I honestly wasn't sure if they were dreams or reality.

"Oliver does all the cooking at the manor,

and he or Henry would happily make your tea for you. Most of the time I prefer to make it myself. I find something soothing about the process."

She opened a cupboard that revealed more tea options than most stores stocked.

Lisa turned to me with a grin. "Ah... so do you want me to give you the options? That could take a while."

With wide eyes, I shook my head. "I'm not mean enough to make you read all those labels. Just close your eyes and pick one. I'm yet to meet a tea I don't like."

Chuckling, she put one hand over her eyes while she reached into the cupboard to pull out a container.

"Looks like we're having wine tea. I've had this one before, and it's delicious. Henry told me it's made in Georgia."

Tucking up one leg under my other, I got comfortable on the chair. "I've never had it before, but let's give it a whirl."

Several minutes later, Lisa finished flitting around the room, and we were both sitting down to steaming cups of wine tea.

I cautiously took a sip then hummed at

the mellow grape flavor. "Hmm. This is good."

Lisa took a mouthful of her own drink then set it down and settled a serious look on me.

"You looked rather flustered when you arrived. What did you want to ask me?"

To give myself a little time, I sipped more tea before I set my cup down. I wasn't sure how to even start this conversation.

"Do you mind if I ask you a personal question?"

Her eyes widened a moment before she smiled gently at me. "Of course, you can. I was rather hoping we'd become friends over the coming months. I'm the only female here at the moment, and it gets lonely. The brothers aren't exactly the chatty type."

Brothers. So there were more males than just Cole who lived here. Part of me relaxed as my hopes rose that Cole wasn't Lisa's baby daddy.

"Who's the father of your baby? And does he live here?"

Now it was Lisa's turn to pick up her tea to take another sip. She stayed quiet for a moment before she settled her cup back on the saucer.

"I like that you're direct and don't beat around the bush. Let me guess... Cole followed you home after your interview, didn't he? And naturally, he wouldn't have told you much."

I nodded, fear clogging my throat.

She reached over and clasped my hand in hers. "Cole is not the father. His brother, Noah, is. All the siblings are cursed in a similar fashion but are not exactly the same. After their mother died young, their father had a witch cast a spell on all of his children so they'd never die. Not sure what he thought would happen, but I like to think he didn't plan on them all ending up ghost monsters after they suffered a mortal death. Noah died in a fire, so he's now a big red guy who's very hot-blooded. I don't know the stories of the others, but I've seen Cole, and would guess he drowned."

That had me leaning forward. "Wait. You said you've seen Cole? How?"

Lisa cocked her head to the side. "They have two forms. Well, three if you count their warrior form, but that only comes out if they need to fight. You may never see that version of him. Did Cole not show himself to you? Their main two forms are their monster and ghost ones. And now that I'm mated with Noah, I can see them in their ghost forms too. Not that it stops Noah from sneaking up on me. Those men are insatiable once they find their woman."

Her expression turned dreamy while my own cheeks heated with the memory of how I'd spent the previous night. Tingles ran up my spine a moment before Lisa's gaze focused over my shoulder and a grin lit her face.

"Speaking of the devil."

I looked over but couldn't see anything, not even an outline or any distortion.

"I am no devil."

Oh, I knew that deep voice. I tried to hold in the shudder as I remembered all the wicked things that voice had led me to do last night.

Lisa rolled her eyes. "It's a figure of speech, Cole. I wasn't calling you a devil. Geez." She rose from her seat, running a palm over her slightly rounded belly. "Well, I'll leave you two to it. Cole, tell her everything. No matter how unimportant you think it is, know it isn't to Katherine. You need more than great sex between the two of you if you want to keep her."

I ignored her departure and continued to scan the room, straining my eyes, trying to find him.

"You won't be able to see me in this form unless I fully claim you as my mate."

It was beyond strange trying to talk to someone I couldn't see. "Lisa said you have two forms. I can see you if you take your monster form, right?"

He was quiet for a moment before his rich voice filled the air again. "Yes. But you'll need to come to my pond if you want me to show you."

Giving up trying to find where he was, I stared into my teacup, lifting it to swirl the remaining liquid. "Why can't you just show me here?"

"A few reasons. As you have no doubt already worked out, I have tentacles. In my monster form, they dry out quickly if I'm not submerged. I will also make the floor wet, and Henry has enough to do without having to follow me around, cleaning up after me."

The mental image of Henry following behind a half octopus, half man with a mop and bucket had me smiling as I lifted my tea to finish it off.

"Well, since I don't want to make more work for anyone, I guess we're going to your pond." Standing, I moved across the room to put my cup in the sink. "How are you going to lead me when I can't see you?"

"I could carry you, or I can simply give you instructions."

My body heated up in an instant at the thought of him carrying me because I knew he would not keep his hands — or tentacles — to himself.

I cleared my throat, but my voice still came out a little breathy. "Ah, I think verbal commands might be safer for the moment."

His low laugh surrounded me, and I grew slick enough to soak my panties. Fingers gripped then tugged on both my nipples, and with a moan, I reached behind me to grab the counter to stop myself from sliding to the floor.

"Where's the fun in being safe? There's

no rush to get to my pond. Not when you smell so delicious."

A tentacle slid up the inside of my calf, under my skirt and I shuffled my feet as far as the fabric would allow to give him room to keep moving up to my wet panties.

"Is all this cream for me, *la sirena*?"

I nodded then shuddered when my panties slid down my legs. Without him needing to say a word, I stepped out of them, and he whisked them away. With another sexy growl, he shoved up my skirt until it was bunched around my waist. Less than a heartbeat later, my legs were shoved wide, and his slick tongue lapped over my aching pussy, making me moan his name.

Sparks shot through my entire body when he sucked on my clit while a tentacle slid inside my pussy. Just like last night, he lined up a suction cup with my G-spot and latched on. My body shook with instant overload, and my fingers slipped off the counter behind me. Before I could crumple to the floor, tentacles surrounded my waist and calves, holding me suspended in midair. If someone walked in right now, I'm sure I'd look a sight, floating along with my pussy on full display. The thought made me hotter.

Two more tentacles slipped under my shirt and bra, latching suction cups onto each nipple as his tongue continued to work magic on my clit. He already had me worked up enough that I was on the edge of a massive climax and whimpered while I bucked my hips against his face. Then another tentacle slid between my ass cheeks, finding my rear entrance, where it teased and circled the tight muscle there until it loosened and allowed him to thrust that slick appendage deep into my back passage. It lit up all sorts of nerve endings, and it was exactly what I needed to tip over the edge.

"Cole!"

The edges of my vision went dark as a massive orgasm rolled through me. The bliss of shattering apart so completely consumed me, stealing my breath and sanity. I was a limp doll as Cole wound more tentacles around me to hold me securely before we began to move from the kitchen. A shiver ran over me as I seemingly floated through the air unaided. I probably should be more bothered by the strange sensation, but I didn't have the energy to wrap my head around it, so I just closed my eyes with a sigh and enjoyed my post-orgasm bliss for as long as I could.

FOUR

COLE

MY GHOST FORM was a complex thing. I could choose to fully be a spirit, able to float through walls or any other solid matter, unable to be felt or to feel anything or anyone. Or I could choose to make certain parts of me feel solid while remaining invisible. That was how I could fuck my pretty little siren while in my ghost form. It was also how I could carry her limp form from the kitchen to my bed of moss at the rear of my pond.

Before laying her down, I stripped off the rest of her clothes, caressing her soft skin as I did. I knew as soon as she came down from her orgasm high, she'd want me to show her my monster form and I prayed she wouldn't reject me. Fear paralyzed me at the thought I wouldn't ever be able to touch her again.

My cock throbbed as she reached her arms over her head and arched her back in a full body stretch that had her tits pushing up, the rosy tips hard in the cool air.

"Hmm."

Her pale skin against the green of the moss held me mesmerized. In that instant, I knew without a doubt, I could stare at this woman forever and never tire of the sight. Sitting up, she rubbed her eyes before scanning around her.

"Cole?"

"I'm here, *la sirena.*"

"This is your pond, right?"

I knew what she was going to ask next, and it had my muscles tensing as I tried to think of a way to put off the inevitable.

"Yes. You're laying where I sleep."

Her unusually dark blue eyes, so similar in color to the deepest part of the lake outside, continued to scan the room as she spoke. "So you'll show me what you look like now?"

With a sigh, I moved to the end of the bed, taking a moment to memorize everything about her in case she changed her mind after she saw me. Then, without taking my gaze off her face, I shifted forms.

"Oh, wow."

With wide eyes, she scanned me from the tip of my horns down to my tentacles. Nerves had me lifting a palm to rub over my chest. Her gaze followed my hand.

"You're blue and purple."

I nodded, not sure what to say.

"Can I touch you?"

My breath caught at her question, and I cocked my head. "You're not repulsed by me in this form?"

Unlike Noah, who'd remained mostly human looking, I had fucking tentacles instead of legs. Noah's mate hadn't rejected me when she'd seen me in my monster form, but it was easier to accept someone you didn't spend a whole lot of time with. Especially after they helped to save your life.

My Katherine's smile was like sunshine in the middle of winter as she began to crawl toward me. "Babe, I'd already figured out you had tentacles. Little hard to miss those even when I couldn't see what you were touching me with."

By the time she was kneeling in front of me, I was panting with need and clenching my fists, so I didn't reach for her. This was too good to be true. Not only had she not rejected me, but she was willingly coming closer. I might actually have a real chance at keeping her.

I hissed when she placed both palms on my chest, her touch lighting up nerves long neglected. When she didn't back away from my bared fangs but instead slid her hands up to my shoulders, I couldn't hold back another moment. Wrapping my arms around her waist, I pulled her in tight against me and buried my face in her neck as I shook with the intensity of what I was feeling. Hope, relief, the beginnings of love... they all swirled within me like never before.

"Oh, sweetheart. I'd never be so shallow as to reject someone for how they look. I learned very young to not judge a book by its cover. I was raised at Blackwell Retreat, surrounded by men, women and children who had been horribly hurt in the past.

Some of them have terrible scars but are the loveliest of people."

My hold tightened. "Were you hurt? Before you went to the retreat?"

She rubbed her face against my shoulder, causing a shiver to run down my spine. "My father was a drunk and would beat my mom. I was a baby when she left him and moved to Blackwell. I don't even remember what he looks like, let alone anything he might have done to me." She paused for a moment. "He's dead now. I overheard William telling Mom that he'd died in a car accident."

Relief she hadn't been abused and he was no longer alive to come after her had me easing my grip on her, but it was several minutes before I had myself under control enough to fully loosen my hold and straighten up. Her smile was gentle, and I managed to hold in my wince at the look in her eyes. Pity wasn't the emotion I wanted from my woman.

Dammit, I was an Alpha male. A monster with all sorts of tricks up my sleeve. Pushing aside the last of the emotion that had caught me off guard, I slid a palm up her back until I could tangle my fingers in her hair. Tightening my hold, I took control of her and the situation. Tilting her head back, I lowered my mouth to cover hers, delving my tongue in when she gasped.

With a light touch, she cupped my face as I continued to kiss her deeply. When she slid her hands up and ran her fingers over my horns, my entire body jerked as my cock throbbed. My tentacles parted to allow my erection to spring free. When I rubbed my hard length against her stomach, she gasped and tightened her grip, making me groan. My horns were nearly as sensitive as my dick. She began to stroke my horns, chuckling when I shivered.

"Guessing you like your horns stroked, huh?"

"Very much so."

Removing one hand, she wriggled until she had room to lower it down to wrap her fingers around my cock, and I bucked with a hiss of pleasure.

"But I bet you like this even more."

Unlike my brothers, I didn't make it a regular habit to go visiting women in their sleep. With how I was limited by how much time I could spend away from the water here at the manor, I hadn't often bothered heading out to find relief from the constant sexual ache that was part of our curse. I could barely remember the last time I'd touched a woman before Katherine. And none had ever touched me. I'd stayed in my ghost form. Letting the females believe they were dreaming. Katherine's warm hands on my flesh had me realizing how starved for affection and touch I was. That she would continue to touch me so willingly after seeing my monster form was more than I'd ever dared to even dream of.

Cupping her face, I stared into her eyes, soaking in the arousal and lust there.

"You are a treasure. Utter perfection."

Before she could respond, I pressed my lips to hers again. Being careful of my fangs once more so I didn't nick her tender flesh, when she opened her mouth, I deepened the kiss. By the time I pulled back, my tentacles were wrapped around her legs and waist, holding her firmly in my grip.

Her wide grin and the sparkle in her eyes had my heart skipping a beat.

"That was some kiss, babe. But I

wouldn't mind kissing you in other, more interesting places."

Before I could ask what she meant, she was leaning in to kiss my chest, stroking both palms over my abs before she gripped my hips and kissed her way lower. My breath hitched and my pulse kicked up speed when she kept going down. Would she really be so adventurous this soon?

I had to be the luckiest monster on the planet because yes, she was.

With a hand wrapped around the base, she swiped her tongue over the head of my cock, taking the bead of precum. My body was nearly vibrating with pleasure, especially when she hummed and went back for more.

Stretching her lips wide, she took me inside the warmth of her mouth. In my monster form, I was slightly larger than when I was a ghost, so I was too big for her to take much of me, but I didn't care. She stroked both hands up and down my length while she alternated between sucking and swirling her tongue round the head. All the while she kept her gaze locked on mine. No matter how hard I looked, I couldn't see any trace of repulsion or pity. Only lust and desire. This woman humbled me.

Threading my fingers into her soft, wavy, reddish-orange hair, I surrounded her with my tentacles, wrapping her up until she couldn't escape, not that she appeared to want to leave. Then I let the tips wander. When I slipped one between her thighs and up until it was buried within her slick sheath, she moaned around my cock, nearly making me come before I was ready to end this little game.

Fucking her pussy with one tentacle, I traced the tip of another down her spine until I reached the rosette of her back entrance. I rimmed her until the muscle relaxed, making penetration possible. As I began to thrust in and out of her ass, I placed suction cups on both her nipples and her clit.

The moment I began to stimulate all her pretty pink bits at once, her eyes widened, and her body began to shake. She hummed around my cock, and I couldn't hold off, not when she was about to shatter completely apart for me.

"Swallow me down, *la sirena*. Don't you waste a drop."

The urge to mark her again was overwhelming. I needed to fill her belly, then her womb and her ass with my seed. Then I'd coat her skin with my cum again until there was no question who she belonged to. I wasn't happy that she'd washed off all my shimmer from where I'd marked her last night. Later, once I'd worn us both out completely, I'd explain why it was important she didn't do that.

KATHERINE

When I could focus again after another massive orgasm, I was lying on my back with Cole over me. There was a look of wonder in his gaze that broke my heart. Lifting my palm, I cupped his cheek.

"Why do you expect to be rejected?"

"Because I am a monster."

Tears pricked my eyes at his simple answer. "Looking different shouldn't be the mantel of your soul. Your actions should be. I'd never reject you over how you looked."

I'd heard so many stories at the retreat of how perfect residents' partners had appeared. Seemed to me it was often the most handsome of men and prettiest of women who had evil deep inside. He opened his mouth, but no words came out, as though I'd left him speechless. Turning his head, he pressed a kiss to my palm.

"You humble me, *la sirena.*"

I shrugged as I let my hand lower back down to rest beside me while embarrassment left me feeling uneasy. Running my palms over the soft moss helped ground me as I tried to blow off the compliment. "Just saying how I see it."

"It's how you see it that's special. That will always be special to me."

I had no idea how to respond to him, but he didn't give me time to flounder. He lowered down and pressed his lips to mine, emptying my mind of all thoughts other than the pleasure he could bestow on me.

Breaking the kiss, he smiled as he glanced down at my naked body. "Hmm, all mine."

He surrounded me, touching me with his hands and tentacles. My entire being hummed with arousal at the overload of stimulation.

"Cole." Groaning his name, I reached to run my palms over the closest two tentacles. When I caught a suction cup, he shuddered, making me grin.

"Are they sensitive?"

I ran a fingertip around a larger one while he shook his head. "More ticklish than sensitive. No one's ever touched them before."

With a smirk, I raised an eyebrow his way.

He rolled his eyes. "*La sirena*, I've used them to touch others, not the other way around. No one has even tried before you."

That made my heart hurt for him. "No one's ever given you any affection?"

His gaze locked onto my breasts as he used his fingers to toy with my nipples, elongating them.

"My brothers have always been there for me. They're monsters too, so they don't wince at my tentacles. And when Lisa was fleeing a stalker, she ended up in my pond, so I held her to keep her safe until her mate came to rescue her. She didn't reject me, but she also didn't reach for me like you do."

A kernel of jealousy rose within me. "I'm glad she didn't. Let's keep it that way."

He grinned then lowered his face toward my chest. "I like that you're possessive. I am too. I would become very angry if another male touched you."

Before I could assure him that no man could compare to him, he took my right nipple into his mouth and gave it a hard suck.

"Oh, damn."

He'd made the tips so sensitive with his fingers that the suction of his mouth lit them up like never before. He did the same thing to the left before he wrapped his hands around my breasts, pushing them together so he could get both nipples into his mouth at the same time. I ran my fingers through his long hair as he set about tormenting the hell out of my breasts.

He stiffened when I shifted to grip his horns but didn't stop. Wanting to return at least some of the pleasure he was giving me, I started to stroke his horns, twisting my hands around them as though they were his cock. He moaned against my nipples a moment before the broad head of his erection pressed against my entrance.

When I had my mouth on him, I'd realized he was larger in this form, and he proved it again as a delicious burn lit me up while he slowly buried himself inside me. I loved being full. No man or toy had ever filled me up or satisfied me like Cole. Planting my feet on the moss, I pushed my hips up to take him deeper, moaning when he pressed up against my cervix.

He lifted his head enough to look at me. "You like a touch of pain with your pleasure, *la sirena?*"

I groaned out my answer as he bottomed out again. "Love it."

Lowering back down, he timed his hard sucks on my nipples with his thrusts into me, and I followed his rhythm with my hands on his horns, speeding up when he did.

He slipped a tentacle between my legs and up to my ass, teasing my back entrance for a few moments before he penetrated me.

With a scream that echoed around the room, I shattered apart for the third time. My back passage clenched down on the tentacle while my sheath pulsed around his thick cock that continued to thrust in and out of me until with a groan, he came, and warmth filled my womb.

I was still floating on my orgasm high when he pulled out of my pussy, wrapped a tentacle around my waist to lift my ass up and replaced the tentacle with his dick. The burn was almost too much, I pulled fistfuls of moss out as I tried to adjust to the massive cock invading my back passage.

A suction cup sealed over my clit, pulsing against the sensitive nub in a way that had my entire body loosening, then a tentacle slipped inside my pussy, fucking me while his cock sank deeper into my ass.

"So good, *la sirena*."

As he moaned the words, he leaned forward and once more began to torment my nipples and breasts with his mouth and hands. The burn of him sinking deeper mixed with arousal and before I knew it, I was panting on the edge coming again. Reaching up, I gripped his horns as my body shattered apart. For a moment, I worried I'd never be whole again, but then darkness took over my vision and all thoughts vanished.

As I returned to consciousness, warm liquid splattered over my chest and stomach. By the time I was awake enough to speak, he was rubbing his cum over my skin.

"Don't you make me sparkle again, Cole. That's a hard limit."

He paused and frowned up at me. "Hard limit?"

I reached out to grab his wrists when he resumed spreading his seed. "Yes. Meaning something I'm not budging on. You can't make my skin shimmer like I'm going out for a night on the town every time we have sex!"

I sighed when his tentacles took over the task since I held his hands. I guess he had a hard limit of his own on this particular subject.

"But I need to mark you, to make sure that everyone who sees you knows that you're claimed and to keep their hands off."

He was so frustratingly possessive. I wished I didn't find that so damn sexy. "Babe, you need to trust me that I only want you and won't allow anyone else to touch me."

He frowned, looking adorable, although I wasn't going to tell him that. I'm sure he thought he looked fierce.

"It's not you I don't trust, *la sirena*. It's all the other men. You're a beautiful woman, and you're mine alone. I don't share."

That had me chuckling. "I caught that about you. There's no other lover in my life. I'm pretty much alone now that I'm living in Batsonville. My mom lives at the retreat, and William, the man who owns it, has been like a father to me but like my mom, doesn't leave the retreat much either."

An image of Ash flashed through my mind, making me frown.

"Who did you just think of?"

There was a possessive growl to Cole's tone that I didn't want to like.

"No one you need to worry about. Let's just say I don't miss everybody from the retreat now that I'm living away from it."

His expression softened, and he leaned down to press a gentle kiss to my lips, the motion so tender, my chest ached for a few moments.

"Well, you're not alone anymore. Lisa will be your friend and sister. You can move into the manor, and this will be your new home. You'll like it here. I'll make sure you're happy."

Such a dictator. I reached up to cup his face between my palms. "Cole, you can't just declare that. I hope I do form a friendship with Lisa, but for the moment, she and Noah are my employers. And I'm not ready to move out here. Lisa suggested it too, but I don't know any of you well enough yet. I don't need to live here to do my job."

He smirked, a sparkle of humor in his black eyes. "You know, Lisa started as an employee of the Manor too."

I rolled my eyes but couldn't hold in the smile. The more time I spent with my monster, the more I grew to like all the sides of him. Even that caveman side.

"Of course, she did." Pressing a palm against his chest, I smiled up at my possessive monster. "I can't stay in bed all day. I need to go home and get my laundry done, food shopping—"

He cut me off with a growl and glared

down at me. "I don't like it. I can't go with you."

Lifting my other palm, I started running my hands over his muscular chest, unable to resist the temptation of his soft skin.

"You followed me home yesterday. Why can't you do it again today?"

His hands returned to my breasts, his nimble fingers toying with my nipples, sending waves of arousal through me despite the ache between my legs that told me I needed to have a little recovery time.

"It's part of my curse. I need the water here in my pond, or the lake behind the manor. I can only leave for a short time. If I leave for as long as I did last night, I must spend the next couple of days here."

My heart ached for him. "You mean you're basically trapped here?"

The manor was huge, but no building was large enough to be someone's whole world.

He shrugged a shoulder before lowering himself down to run his tongue over a nipple.

"It's not so bad. With you here, I can't imagine anywhere else I'd rather be."

When he repeated the attention to my other breast, I knew I needed to distract him or my ravenous monster would be inside me again, and I was way too sore for another round right now.

"Will you show me the lake?"

He lifted up to frown down at me. "You don't want me to touch you?"

My poor monster had an insecurity issue. I reached up to cup his face between my palms.

"Cole, I'm pretty sure I'm going to crave your touch for all time, but my body needs a break. I've had more sex in the last twenty-four hours than I've had in a damn long time. And I've never had a lover as well-endowed as you. You gotta give me some recovery time between rounds, babe."

A broad grin stretched over his face.

"So, you're saying I'm the best you've ever had?"

I rolled my eyes. Such a male. "Yes, my ravenous ghost monster. You're such a spectacular lover that I need breaks between rounds so I don't expire from the overload of awesomeness."

"Smart ass."

He covered my lips with his, kissing me deeply, and by the time he lifted away, I was wondering if I was really that sore after all.

"Come on, *la sirena*. Get dressed and I'll show you some of the manor, then the lake."

CHAPTER
FIVE

COLE

AFTER I WENT to gather her clothes, and she covered her delicious body, we left my pond room. I turned ghost so as not to make a mess everywhere we went. It also meant Katherine couldn't see me staring at her the entire way. Keeping my focus on her was much better than thinking about the lake and what had happened there so many years ago.

"This is my wing of the manor. You're welcome to explore any room here, and you can redecorate however you'd like. Well, except for my pond room. I need that just how it is. Head in this door on your left."

Aside from visiting the kitchen to eat, the

only other room in the manor I really used or cared about was my pond room. Although, once Katherine moved in, there'd be one more room I would spend a lot of time in.

Following my directions, she turned into the room right next to my pond.

"This one room is bigger than my entire apartment!"

"This is your suite of rooms. The bathroom is over to your right and a large walk-in wardrobe is the closed door next to the bathroom."

With her mouth hanging open and her eyes wide, she did a slow turn, taking in the space. I followed her gaze and tried to see what she was seeing. The manor had always been my home. Even when I'd been human, I hadn't gone off exploring like my siblings.

The room was like all the other bedrooms in the manor. Large floor-to-ceiling windows and French doors along the outside wall were draped in heavy silk curtains. The large four-poster bed was covered in an elegant bedspread with big, fluffy pillows just waiting for my Katherine to rest her head on. The sitting area of the room had a Persian rug and delicate antique chairs I'd never be able to risk sitting in. The large fireplace was cold and empty, but once she moved in, I'd make sure it was cracking with a soothing fire whenever she desired. This old stone manor could get damn cold in the winter. It was why once the technology was available, heaters were added to my pond water.

"This is too much, Cole! I can't live here. I'd be too worried about breaking something valuable to risk touching anything."

Her voice was barely a whisper and the need to soothe her overtook me. I rushed forward and switched to my monster form as I reached her, wrapping myself around her, encasing her in my arms and tentacles, holding her against my chest.

"Nothing in this manor is worth more than you, *la sirena*. So long as you don't break yourself, no one will care about anything else here. If you don't like the furniture or any other items, we can replace them with more modern things.

She wrapped her arms around my neck and buried her face against my throat.

"I'm still dreaming, aren't I?"

I chuckled at that as I ran my hand over

her head, letting my fingers glide through her thick, red wavy hair.

"I'm no dream, Katherine."

Emotion clogged my throat as I struggled with what to say. After embracing her for a few more moments I loosened my hold, wanting to break this melancholy mood that had fallen over us both.

"How about we head outside and see the lake? Do you like roses?"

She cleared her throat as though she too was struggling with emotions that were too close to the surface.

"Who doesn't like roses?"

I shrugged. "They do have thorns, so I'm sure some people don't like them."

With a smile that lit up the room she laughed. "Good thing I don't mind pretty things that can bite me, huh?"

She winked my way before strolling out of the room and down the hallway.

Shaking my head at her quirky sense of humor, I turned ghost and followed after her, guiding her out of the manor and toward the lake I normally avoided.

While Katherine strode right up to the lake, I slowed my pace. My heart began to race the closer I got as memories assailed me like they always did when I came here. With a wince, I forced myself to stand beside my woman on the southern shore, a few of my tentacles automatically reaching for the water I needed to survive as I stared over at the east side where I'd died. Even while my mind was caught in pain, my body began to strengthen from being in contact with the lake's water.

"Even though I can't see you, I can feel your pain. Why did you bring me here if it hurts so much?"

"You wanted to see it, so I showed you."

She huffed. "Your ghost form can be very frustrating. I want to hold you, comfort you, but I can't."

With a smile, I switched forms, loving that even in this place, Katherine could brighten my mood. The moment I was visible, she turned and moved forward to embrace me. I wrapped my arms and a few tentacles around her, holding her as close as I could, then lowered my face to her hair, breathing in her sweet Ghost Orchid scent.

"This is where I died and activated the curse."

Her grip on me tightened but she stayed silent. Somehow her quiet acceptance and support had my mouth moving when normally I didn't speak much, especially about this.

"I was thirty-seven years old and way too arrogant for my own good. Raised with privilege, I'd been quite sure nothing could take me down. Even after losing our mother in a boating accident, I'd not really thought about my own mortality.

"The moment Tarquin, my horse, had decided to do his own thing while we were exploring the land around the manor, that changed. Once that damn horse took off and refused to obey any of my commands, I was definitely thinking about how easily I could get hurt or die. In hindsight, I suspect he saw a snake or some other critter that had spooked him, but that didn't make a lick of difference to the outcome. He'd been at a full out sprint until he came to the lake, where he skidded to a halt to prevent himself from going into the water. While he managed to save himself, I'd flown straight out of the saddle and into the bloody water."

I lifted my gaze to the east side again.

The manor's lake only had a small area on the southern side that was a sandy shore and easy access to and from the water. The rest of it was surrounded with boulders and small cliffs that led into the extremely deep water.

"Unfortunately for me, Tarquin threw me in over there, on the eastern side where the water is damn deep. I'd never learned to swim, and I was too far away from the edge to be able to reach it."

A shudder ran through me as I remembered the burn of inhaling water as I drowned. You'd think after a couple of hundred years, the memories would fade, and many had. But those surrounding my death were still vivid.

Katherine pressing a soft kiss over my heart pulled my mind back to the present. I cupped her face, tilting her head up so I could press my mouth to hers, kissing her deeply and with all the emotion that was roiling inside me.

This woman was the calm in my storm, and I hated that I was going to have to let her leave soon. I wanted, no, *needed* her with me.

When I broke the kiss, her lids were low, and she panted for breath looking so damn sexy, I wanted nothing more than to get inside her again. But she was sore from our earlier games, and I doubted she'd want to be thrown down on the grass, out in the open, for me to devour her.

"Stay with me."

She reached up and stroked her hand down the side of my face as her gaze turned sad.

"I have to go. It's way too soon for me to move in. I will admit, I'm falling hard for you, Cole, but I can't rush in to moving in here. I need to be careful."

While I could understand the sense in what she was saying, I hated the logic. I knew in the depths of my soul that she was destined to be my mate, to be beside me forever.

"Know that I'll be waiting for the moment you are ready. And until you move in, you can come visit every day. I don't care how often Lisa needs you to work with her, I need you every day."

She chuckled and lifted up to press a quick kiss to my lips.

"Such a ravenous ghostie."

KATHERINE

Only after the sun started to set and the air grew chilly did I manage to force myself to leave the manor. The drive back to my apartment was quiet, and Henry seemed to understand I didn't want to chat. I chewed my thumbnail as I contemplated my options. Both Lisa and Cole had offered for me to move out to the manor now. When Lisa had offered, it had felt wrong, too fast. But when Cole had mentioned it today, I'd wanted nothing more than to agree.

That was crazy, right? One thing that had been drummed into me growing up at the retreat was that you didn't rush into things with a partner, and the more perfect they seemed, the more careful you should be. Although, as much as I thought Cole was perfect, he didn't see himself that way. He'd honestly been scared I'd reject him for how he looked. Surely, he could work out that if I didn't have an issue with him being a ghost, I wouldn't have one with him being able to turn into a monster.

Before I could finish processing my thoughts, we pulled up to my apartment.

"Thanks, Henry. Guess I'll be seeing you tomorrow."

He smiled. "It would certainly make Cole a happy man if you did, Miss Turner."

I laughed at that. "Call me Katherine, Henry. And I'll see you tomorrow at ten."

"See you then, Katherine."

Then he drove off, and I headed toward the front of my apartment building. My mood took an instant nosedive when I entered the lobby area to find Ash pacing.

"Ash? What on earth are you doing here?"

He spun my way and rushed to stand in front of me.

"This place is a fucking dump, babe. You're not staying here. Go get your shit, and I'll take you back home where you belong."

Anger rose quickly at his words.

"You have no right to tell me what to do, Ash. None. I'm staying here because it's cheap, and I didn't want to waste retreat money unnecessarily. Now I have a job and can pay my own way. I'll decide when I want to move out. Not you. Not anyone."

He rolled his eyes and with a huff reached to grab my wrist. "Stop being stupid. Let's go get your shit."

"Ash, stop it. You're hurting me."

His grip tightened and his eyes narrowed, but before he could say anything else, a new voice spoke up. "Is this man giving you trouble, Katherine?"

Tylah Huie was the building manager who lived in the apartment closest to the lobby. I'd only met him a few times and would have doubted he'd remember my name, but I was glad he had thought to intervene. He was probably six feet two and clearly knew where the local gym was. Ash wasn't a slouch. He worked on the farm portion of the retreat and was strong, but he was only five feet eleven and looked scrawny in comparison.

Now that Ash was focused on Tylah, I managed to twist my wrist free from his grasp and take a few steps away.

"Yeah, Mr. Huie, he's trying to get me to leave against my will."

At my words, Tylah moved closer, and as Ash puffed up for the oncoming confrontation, I dashed to stand behind my landlord, feeling safer with his big body between me and Ash.

"Why don't you head into my apartment, Katherine, while I deal with this problem for you."

It didn't sit right to let someone else—a virtual stranger—deal with my problems, but I was physically tired after my big day and mentally worn out after trying to figure out if I should be trying to slow things down with Cole, or just roll with the way they were happening.

Before passing through Tylah's door, I turned to face Ash. "Just do us all a favor and go home, Ash. Maybe talk to William about your attitude toward women, because with how we were raised, you should know better."

Pain flickered over his face, and he stepped toward me. "Katherine, don't—"

Tylah cut him off with a shove to his chest. "I don't think so, buddy. You need to head off."

Turning my back on the men, I went into Tylah's apartment and collapsed down onto his couch. With a sigh, I scrubbed my palms over my face, struggling to believe this was currently my life. Who the hell did Ash think he was? How the hell had he listened to all the stories the women and men had told at the retreat and still believe women were possessions?

"Well, he's now gone." The sound of tires squealing accompanied his words until he closed the door and shut the sound out. "Want a tea or coffee before you head up to your apartment?"

Feeling numb, I nodded. "Tea would be great, thanks."

"Cream or sugar?"

"No cream and one sugar, please."

He disappeared into the kitchen, and I sat back, closing my eyes for a minute. Before I knew it, Tylah was back with two mugs.

"Here you go."

Forcing a smile, I took the offered tea. "Thank you, for the drink and for stepping in. Not too many people would interfere in someone else's problems."

He shrugged a shoulder before he sat on a single armchair opposite where I was seated. "I'm the caretaker of this building, that includes the people who live here. Drink your tea, it'll help."

Taking a deep breath, I relaxed my shoulders and lifting the cup, began to sip at the hot liquid. It was just plain black tea, but I still found it soothing, and by the time I'd finished the cup, I was feeling much calmer. Leaning forward, I reached to set my empty mug down on the coffee table, but suddenly my head spun and there were two tables.

"What—" my voice slurred, and dizziness filled my mind.

The cup was taken from my hands. "You're not looking so good, Katherine. I think you need to lie down."

He scooped me up from the couch, and I was limp in his grip. I couldn't move my arms or legs. My head fell against his chest while panic overtook my thoughts. Bastard had drugged my tea. He must have.

Focusing all my remaining energy on my eyes, I kept them open as he took me deeper into his apartment and into a room with padded walls. Laying me down on a bed, he stroked my cheek.

"Been watching you, girl. Wanted you for a while now. Ain't gonna turn down this chance to have you. And to think you just walked into my lair willingly. I ain't ever letting you go. He opened a drawer on the nightstand and then he had a syringe in his hand.

"But your timing is shit, babe. I gotta go out tonight, so it's sleep time for you till morning. Tomorrow will be soon enough for me to finally get a taste of you."

Tears leaked from my eyes, but I couldn't move an inch. I let my lids close as the needle slipped into my flesh. An image of Cole filled my mind, and I knew now I should have accepted the offer to move out to the manor immediately. My last thought before I slipped into unconsciousness was a prayer that I'd see my ghost monster again.

CHAPTER
SIX

COLE

After waking this morning, I'd ghosted out to the lake again, submerging myself in the cold water so I could be as recharged as possible to allow me to go home with Katherine when she left the manor today. Henry had departed a while ago to go collect her, and the moment she arrived, I'd go to her.

"You back to normal yet, brother?"

I jerked in surprise as Noah appeared on the shore in front of me in his ghost form. It was unlike him to come seek me out when I was in the water, so I was instantly on alert.

"Why? What's happened?"

"Henry returned without Katherine. He said she wasn't waiting for him, and when he went inside and knocked on her door, there was no answer."

In one fluid movement, I was on the shore beside my brother.

"What do you mean, she wasn't there?"

Fear had my tentacles twitching.

Noah frowned at me. "She didn't answer the door when Henry knocked."

"Something must have happened to her. Where's Henry? I need to go to her."

Noah stuck by my side as we headed toward the manor.

"Did you want me to come with you? If she's changed her mind about you, we can both use our voices on her to get her to at least reconsider continuing with the job. That will have her here at the manor so you can woo her."

I shook my head. "She wouldn't change her mind. She feels the connection as much as I do. She's nervous about how fast it's happening, but not about me. She didn't even flinch when she saw my monster form. No, something's happened."

"Well, either way, I think I'll come with you."

Not slowing my pace as we rushed through the manor, I glanced briefly at Noah.

"Why would you leave your pregnant mate to come help me?"

While, as the eldest of us siblings, he'd always looked out for us, leaving Lisa without monster protection, especially when she was pregnant, was out of character for my possessive brother.

Noah smirked. "It's for Lisa that I'm helping. I mean, she's clearly your chosen mate, and I would do anything to help you find the happiness I've found with my Lisa, but she and the baby need Katherine too."

I scoffed. Of course. I'd all but forgotten why Katherine had come to the manor in the first place. As we reached the foyer where Henry was pacing, clearly waiting for Noah to return with me, I looked my brother in the eye and spoke in a voice only ghosts could hear.

"I would appreciate you joining me. Yesterday, she was all in with being with me. Quickly agreed to return today to spend time with me. The only reason she didn't agree to move in when I asked was because she was worried about rushing things. I'm concerned something has happened to her."

Noah took his monster form so Henry could see him. The moment he did, their butler was striding his way.

"I assumed you would want to come with us, so I've sent Oliver to guard Lisa's room. He's armed and will shoot anything that comes his way."

Oliver might be their cook, but he could handle firearms well. He'd spent some time in the military before he'd gone looking for a quieter life and found the manor.

"Thank you, Henry. I was going to ask if he could do just that while we're gone. While I'm not expecting anything to happen, I'd prefer we be prepared just in case. Cole's here, so let's get back to Katherine's and see what we can find out."

When Henry pulled the car up outside Katherine's apartment building, Noah groaned.

"She has as much sense as my Lisa. Why must they stay in such hovels?"

Henry cleared his throat. "Not everyone is born into money, Noah. I'm sure, just like Lisa had, Katherine is doing the best she can with what she has."

I could see Henry's point, but like Noah, I wasn't happy she'd been living in such a place. When I'd first followed her back here, I'd wanted to bundle her up and take her back to the manor. The only thing that stopped me was the fact that I wanted forever with her and didn't want to risk scaring her off.

"She grew up at Blackwell Retreat, so she's very cautious. I suspect the retreat paid for her to train as a doula. If I had to guess, I'd say she selected this place because it was cheap, and she didn't want to burden the retreat with having to pay any more than they absolutely had to." I glanced my brother's way. "Let's float up and check her apartment first."

After calculating which window was Katherine's, Noah followed me as I moved higher and then through the window into her living area. Everything was just as it had been when I'd last been here. Shifting through the small apartment showed there was nothing out of place, no signs of a struggle or break-in. And no sign of her, either. Dread had a firm hold of my heart as we headed back outside and rushed down to join Henry in the limo where we could talk freely.

"She's not there, but all her stuff is. Nothing's been disturbed. Where could she be?"

A man, probably around Katherine's age, marched toward the apartment building's entrance. Before he made it to the door, an older man strode after him, calling out.

"Ash!"

The younger man turned around with a frown but didn't back away from the door.

"Not now, William. I need to go get her. She's not answering my calls."

Turning away from the two men, I frowned at Henry. Since I'd never used a phone in my life – they hadn't existed when I was human – I hadn't considered it. "I hadn't thought of her phone. Did you try to call her?"

Henry nodded but continued to watch the two men outside the car. "Yes. When I was here earlier, I tried, but it went straight to voicemail."

"You need to leave Katherine alone. She is not yours, and even if she were, your behavior is not okay. Have you learned nothing from your mother and the other women?"

The older man, William, saying Katherine's name had my full attention, and I floated out of the vehicle to go stand closer to the men.

Ash got up in William's face, clearly angry. "I learned that I need to make sure I keep what's mine safe. And Katherine isn't safe out in the world. She needs to come home. When I came yesterday, her landlord interrupted us, and she just went into his apartment with no thought! Anything could have happened. And now she's not answering my calls."

William shook his head. "Her phone is off. She's not taking anyone's calls…"

I didn't hang around to listen to more. Fear for my mate's safety had me rushing up the stairs and through the door into the lobby area, Noah on my heels.

Where was the landlord's apartment? I

took a deep breath but couldn't catch Katherine's scent.

Noah spoke as he moved past me, "You take the left, I'll take the right side. Floating through walls, it shouldn't take us long—"

I cut him off when I noticed a sign. "Or we could start with the door that claims that the manager of the building lives inside."

"Or that."

I took a deep breath, bracing myself for whatever we would find inside, then rushed forward and straight through the timber panel. This apartment was larger than Katherine's. At a glance, it looked like it was three bedrooms. The living/kitchen area we stood in was empty and two rooms had open doorways that showed only darkness within. Assuming the bathroom was at the end of the hall, I moved over to the only other closed door and slipped through.

The small bedroom's walls and ceiling were covered in soundproofing and the only furniture was an old metal bed with a bare mattress on it. Noah appeared beside me, hissing as his body grew into his warrior form. My own body thrummed with energy like never before, as though it were readying for battle.

Since I spent so much time avoiding others and rarely left the manor, I'd not ever felt this overwhelming need for vengeance and violence before. When Lisa had taken to my pond to hide from her stalker, I'd felt protective over my brother's woman, but not like this.

Lowering to the floor beside the old, metal-framed single bed where my woman lay unconscious and cuffed, I made myself visible in case she was merely sleeping. The fact she was still fully dressed was a small mercy, but it wouldn't save the man who'd done this to her.

"Katherine? *La sirena*, can you hear me?"

With a moan, she turned her head toward me and blinked open her eyes. Her normally bright dark brown irises were dull and lifeless, the sight punching me in the gut.

"Cole..."

The way she slurred my name left no doubt in my mind that she'd been drugged, but the fact she was alive had a wave of relief flowing through me.

"Where's the one who did this to you?"

I cupped her cheek, and with a hum, she nuzzled into my palm before she seemed to slip back into sleep. Noah moved in close to my side. "You'll need to wait to ask her questions, brother. Break the cuffs off her while I go get Henry to help us get her out to the car. Once she's secure with Henry, we'll come back and look for him."

Noah ghosted out of the room while I remained focused on my woman. With the extra energy buzzing through my blood, snapping the four cuffs took mere moments.

The creak of the door opening had me on full alert. It was too soon for Noah to have made it out to Henry, let alone for the older man to rush inside. Leaving Katherine where she lay, I spun around to face the threat, one of my tentacles slipping over her waist, under her shirt, to make sure she stayed safely behind me. A man I assumed was the building's manager came in and froze when he saw me. With a growl, my body grew in size, filling out to my full warrior form for the first time. My iridescent purple markings began to pulse with a glow, but I didn't let it distract me from watching the one who'd kidnapped my mate.

"Who—" He paused to shake his head. "*What* are you?"

I ran my tongue over my extended fangs, adjusting my mouth to their size so I could talk. "The monster who's going to make you pay for daring to touch Katherine."

With a gulp, he turned to leave, but Noah stood there, his big, red arms folded over his broad chest. In his warrior form, his fangs were out, and his horns gleamed in the light. He looked like the devil, so I wasn't surprised when the scent of urine hit me as the man pissed himself while backing into the room, closer to me. The idiot thought Noah was the bigger threat.

"Make it fast, brother. He's not worth the effort of drawing it out and your woman needs care."

The tentacle I had on her tightened, and a shiver ran through me when her palm slid up the length until she got near the end where it was thin enough for her to wrap her hand around me. My heart warmed that she wanted to keep me close, even when she was barely conscious.

Focusing back on the threat to her, I growled again as I wrapped two of my tentacles around him, covering him from shoulder to knee in seconds. I'd planned to crush him, but before I could tighten the coil, he started screaming in pain, which had me stilling.

Noah had moved into the room and shut the door, keeping any sounds from escaping. "What are you doing to him? End him already."

Panicked, I looked to my brother. "I've never taken this form before, so I have no idea what's happening. I haven't even started to crush him yet."

Noah walked around the man who was now writhing in my grip. Red welts were beginning to rise up on the skin I could see between my tentacles.

"Apparently, you're poisonous in your warrior form. You're stinging him like a Blue Ring Octopus."

Terror filled me as I released the bastard and spun to check on Katherine. I'd never forgive myself if I'd caused her pain.

"What the hell?"

The tentacle she still held in her grip despite being unconscious again wasn't glowing like the rest of me. The iridescent purple markings were their normal shade. Not understanding but not caring so long as she wasn't being hurt, I turned back to the screaming, writhing man on the floor.

The hollering was beginning to hurt my ears, so even though I was tempted to simply leave him in his soundproof room to die slowly, I wrapped one tentacle around his neck and tightened it until he fell silent. A wave of triumph flowed through me at having taken out the threat to my mate, but it was short lived. Concern over the knowledge I was poisonous filled my thoughts.

"Noah, could you please go get Henry so we can all go home? If those two men are still out there, use your voice to get them to leave. I don't want them to see Katherine like this and cause us trouble.

With a nod, my brother ghosted from the room again, and I looked down at my body, willing the glow to recede so I could touch her with my hands.

KATHERINE

With a foggy mind, I rolled over then froze as I realized I was not only in a dark, unfamiliar room, but I was also completely naked.

Where the hell was I? And how did I get here?

I tried to remember what had happened before I went to sleep, but it was all a haze. Movement caught my gaze, and I sat up, clutching the sheets to my chest.

"Who's there?"

A click followed by soft yellow light revealed Lisa. Memories flooded my mind. Lisa and Noah, her ghost monster, were having a baby. They'd offered me a job. Had I forgotten moving out here?

Lisa stood and moved closer. "It's just me, Lisa. You're safe here in your suite of rooms at Gallichan Manor. Do you remember what happened?"

She sat on the edge of the bed, facing me as I shook my head. Tears pricked my eyes as frustration grew.

"Well, from what the guys said, your landlord saved you from a guy from the retreat taking you only to kidnap you himself."

Slamming my eyes closed, I tried to force the memory to surface.

Clenching my fists, I looked up at Lisa. "I can't remember."

"Henry went to pick you up to bring you out here to see Cole, but you weren't there. He came home, then Cole along with Noah decided to go back with him to look for you. Two men from the retreat were there talking. They overheard them mention what had happened last night, so they went in to check the landlord's apartment. They found you cuffed to a bed."

The argument with Ash filled my mind, the way he'd grabbed me and tried to force me out of the building. How Tylah had saved me. My current bedroom morphed into the one at Tylah's apartment, the walls and ceiling soundproofed, like he'd taken other women before me, or had been planning on taking me for some time.

"Ash tried to physically drag me back to

the retreat. Tylah interrupted him and let me hide out in his apartment until Ash left. He gave me tea. Dammit, he must have drugged the tea. He stuck a needle in me. I have no idea what he gave me, but I have short flashes of memory now, like I was in and out of consciousness. I remember Cole, his tentacle over me. Then someone screaming."

I hoped that meant he'd killed Tylah. Taken out the real monster. I'd slipped back out of it before I found out, but I didn't want to ask Lisa.

I shook my head and focused back on her. "Where's Cole?"

She winced. "Shut in his pond room. Our men... they're not used to being accepted. They think they're monsters in the worst sense of the word. Noah told me Cole's scared he could sting you if he gets too emotional and his warrior form comes out. From what Noah said, while he was saving you, was the first time he's ever activated that form."

That had me frowning. "He saved me. He'd never hurt me. I know it in my soul."

Lisa sighed. "Were you awake when it

happened? Like did you actually see everything, or did you just hear it all?"

"I was mostly out of it, but when the screams started, I managed to open my eyes for a few seconds but then I was blacked out again."

She nodded, "So did you see Cole?"

I winced. "Just a blue and purple blur, really. Whatever Tylah gave me really did a number on me."

"Okay, so the ghost monsters have a third form, like a warrior or battle mode. I've seen Noah's. He grows at least a foot and has deadly claws and fangs. According to my mate, Cole's never experienced his warrior form before yesterday. Not sure if you've seen the library here yet, but Noah's always loved researching and reading. He knows a lot about all sorts of bizarre topics. He thinks Cole became poisonous like a Blue Ring Octopus. His purple markings glowed, and when he wrapped his tentacles around Tylah, the man started screaming and his skin came up in red welts."

My head started to pound with everything I was trying to process. "I remember I had one of his tentacles over my body. Why wasn't I stung?"

She shrugged. "As soon as he realized what he was doing, he spun to look at you. Noah said any part of him that was touching you wasn't glowing. You weren't stung. But he wouldn't risk touching you more until all his markings had settled back to normal."

Squinting, I tried to work out what Cole was scared of exactly. "So he's worried about what? That he'll get excited and sting me or something?"

Lisa huffed out a breath as she rolled her eyes. "Men are men, no matter the species. It's all the testosterone, I think. Noah and I will dive deeper into researching how other octopuses use poison, see if we can get more answers, but because the ghost monsters are created with magic, it could be totally different. The fact that he didn't sting you when he was completely enraged has me pretty confident he wouldn't ever sting you. Like you're his mate, and it would be physically impossible for him to harm you. His instincts won't allow it."

An ache lit up within my chest. "But I'm not his mate."

She scoffed at me. "Sure, you're not. All you're missing is his mark. Anyone can see how much you love each other."

Now it was my turn to scoff. "We haven't known each other long enough for talk of love."

She raised an eyebrow as she stared directly at me. "That's why you're upset. Because you don't think he loves you, or that you can't love him so soon. I call bullshit. Love doesn't follow a clock or calendar. It runs on its own time, and when you find the one destined to be yours, you just click. So, when you're feeling up to it, go kick my brother-in-law's ass and claim him."

She got up and strode toward the doorway, a palm over her slightly curved belly as she moved. Before she left, she turned back with a grin. "Oh, one more thing. Welcome to the family, Katherine."

It was only seconds before I was following Lisa out of the room, with nothing but a sheet wrapped around me. Once I was in the hallway, I stilled. Which way was Cole's pond? This manor was massive, I could get lost for a week and not find him. Looking right then left, I was relieved to see the hallway was familiar. I'd been in the room Cole had shown me when he gave me the tour, which meant his pond should be the next room down.

Heading that way, I mentally prepped myself to go kick some monster ass.

SEVEN

COLE

FLOATING in my monster form in the front corner of my pond, I stayed away from my bed that still smelled of Katherine. I didn't deserve a mate, not when I was a poisonous monster with no control.

Unable to stay still, I swam across the pond then back, doing laps to burn off my frustration. I'd put Katherine in her room and tucked her in. Lisa had come and offered to stay with her until she woke, so I'd left and come here. To hide. To rail at a universe that would be so cruel to me yet again. It wasn't enough I was an immortal ghost monster, but I couldn't find solace in a mate either?

The door to my room swung open, and I turned to see who dared to disturb me. Seeing Katherine wrapped in a sheet with her head held high and fire burning in her eyes had me rushing to her on autopilot. I knew I should stay away. It was why I'd left her with Lisa, after all. She deserved the world, not some faulty, poisonous beast. But with her so close, I couldn't stay away. I had to be near her, although I did manage to resist reaching out to touch her.

"What are you doing, Cole?"

I cocked my head to the side. "What do you mean?"

She waved her hands around to indicate the room. "You're hiding in here. Sulking. Why weren't you waiting for me to wake up, to see if I was all right?"

That had me rearing back. "I knew you'd be fine. I could sense your heart rate and life force. I didn't leave you alone. Lisa was with you, so if you did take a turn, she would have called for a doctor. I came here to think."

She clenched the hand not holding the sheet up into a fist as she glared at me. "And what did you decide with all your thinking, Cole?"

Katherine calling me on my shit had me squirming. She really was the most perfect of women.

"I hadn't made any decisions yet."

Her glare deepened into a frown. "What decision were you trying to make?"

"Whether I could leave you alone. I can't risk hurting you, *la sirena*. You deserve so much more than a faulty monster who might sting you every time we touch."

Her expression softened, and she moved toward me. When she dropped the sheet, I hungrily took in her every curve as she moved down the steps into the water. She could easily stand in this end of the pond, so I stayed where I was, letting her come to me. Could she truly still want me?

As soon as she came within my reach, my tentacles automatically surrounded her and drew her in against my chest. Wrapping my arms around her, I held her tightly, knowing instantly I was a fool to ever think I could abandon her. She was part of my heart and soul.

She leaned her face back as she cupped my jaw in her soft palms.

"I deserve to be fully loved for who I am. I

deserve a mate who will always come for me, protect me from anything that would harm me. I deserve to be able to choose for myself who I want. Do you love me, Cole?"

My heart was pounding after her little speech, and I was scarcely able to believe what I was hearing.

"I love you, *la sirena*. You alone own my heart and soul."

She curled her arms around my neck, and I lowered my face down to hers. When there was but a breath between us, she spoke, "And I choose you, Cole. I love every part of you. I know in my soul that you'd never hurt me. From what Lisa said, even when you were completely enraged in your warrior form, whatever parts of you that were touching me stayed harmless." She paused to press a light kiss to my lips. "Claim me as yours. Take me as your mate, Cole."

She'd just offered me everything I'd ever wanted but never dreamed of having. However, I couldn't take it yet. Not without fully explaining what it meant.

"I want to, *la sirena*. More than anything, I want to bind you to me forever. But we need to talk first. I need to let you know everything you'd be agreeing to. Mating is not like marriage—you can't ever break a mate bond."

Scooping her up in my arms, I moved toward the rear of the pond, to my bed. Laying her down on the soft moss, I settled beside her on my side. My tentacles covered her legs, and I stroked my fingers down her arms and across her stomach.

"I know Lisa told you a little about us, but I need to make sure you know everything before you make the decision to mate with me."

She lowered a hand to run over a tentacle, her touch causing a shiver to run through me. I needed to make this history lesson quick, as I wouldn't be able to resist fucking my woman for long.

"I don't remember our mother. I was only a year old when she died in a boating accident. While our father became lost in his grief, Noah became the parent to the rest of us, even though he was only a teen himself. As Lisa told you, our father went to some powerful witches to create a spell to make sure none of his children would die like his wife had. We all lived normal human lives until we suffered a mortal death. After that, we all came back as ghost monsters. In this form, we are immortal, *la sirena*. The witch who created the curse put some extra clauses in that I doubt my father even knew about. One was that each of us could take a mate. That mate would be bound to us forever."

"What about any children? Is Lisa's baby going to be like Noah?"

Fear clogged my throat for a moment, causing my hand to still over her flat tummy.

"We don't know. The twins are off searching for a witch who can give us some answers. We're hoping the baby will be born human, but we can't be sure."

She shook her head. "Why did they risk it?"

"The mating flushed any birth control out of Lisa's system. With how often Noah is on her, it was inevitable he would get her pregnant. And they obviously consider the risk worth it in order to have a baby to love and cherish."

Would she want a baby too? I didn't dare ask in this moment, not when I'd already given her so much to think about. But I knew

I did. I wanted nothing more than to watch Katherine's body swell with our child.

KATHERINE

My heart squeezed in my chest at the look on Cole's face as he pressed his palm over my tummy, over where a child would grow if I were to get pregnant. It was obvious he wanted a baby with me. Could we even complete the mating while preventing pregnancy?

Did I want to prevent it?

I had always wanted kids, a family of my own. Here at the manor, it wouldn't matter if our child was fully human or not. They'd have Lisa's child to grow up with, and they'd always have each other. With Lisa's love of books and research, we'd be able to homeschool them with no problems. And I knew I'd love any children we had. They would be a part of Cole and me, and they would be so very special regardless of whether they were fully human or not. Having grown up at Blackwell Retreat, I knew how to help raise children so they'd be aware of the outside world, along with what not to do, so they'd have all the knowledge they needed if they chose to live away from the manor.

And honestly, the expression of complete adoration and awe on Cole's face while he caressed my stomach was enough to wipe out most of my doubts. A woman would do a lot to keep that look on her man's face.

"What does the mating ritual involve?"

He stilled for a moment. "Are you sure?"

"I'm sure I want you. But I want to know exactly what's going to happen before I'm in one hundred percent."

His tentacles over my legs wrapped tighter around me.

"Sex, blood and cum." He moved down, and I gasped when he teased a nipple with his tongue for a few moments. "While we're having sex, I'll bite you."

Before I realized what he was going to do, he sank his fangs into the side of my breast. But it wasn't pain that shot through my system. No, it was high voltage arousal that had my pussy throbbing with need and a moan rising from my throat.

He hummed as he licked over the wound. "But I won't seal it up with my tongue. I'll use a mix of our cum, and it will create a scar —a mating mark. You'll do the same to me to complete the bond."

Just at him explaining the mating, my body was heating up. As he'd been speaking, one of his tentacles had slipped between my thighs and was very lightly teasing my entrance, sending even more heat through my system.

He moved back up and pressed his lips to mine. A shiver ran down my spine, making me wriggle my hips, trying to get his teasing tentacle in deeper, when a faint hint of copper hit me as he danced his tongue with mine.

We broke apart, and the tentacle teasing me stilled when I reached up to cup his face in my palms.

"I love you, Cole, and I want to be your mate. Claim me and make me yours forever."

He grinned so widely his fangs flashed in the sunlight before he lowered to kiss me again. He was always so careful to not cut or hurt me with his teeth when we kissed. Wrapping my arms around his neck, my heart swelled with love for my monster as he gently took my mouth with a reverent kiss that had goose bumps rising over my entire body.

Leaving my mouth, he kissed his way down to my chin, then up my jawline before he nipped at my ear.

"I love you, Katherine. I've never said those words to another. Only you. I'll make sure you never regret agreeing to be mine."

Before I could think of something to say in response, he kissed his way down my neck. Tentacles wrapped around my wrists and moved my hands up over my head as he reached my breasts.

When he sucked hard on one nipple as he pinched the other, my back arched while I moaned. He alternated between gentle and rough as he took his time teasing my breasts, sending my arousal higher and higher with every movement he made.

"Cole!"

Frustration tinged my voice, and he chuckled as he gave my nipple one last lick.

"You won't rush me, *la sirena*. Not today. I plan to take my time, tasting every part of your luscious body. We're going to make love slowly and thoroughly for the rest of the day and all through the night."

Groaning, he released my hands and moved lower, nipping, licking and kissing his way down my torso, teasing my belly button with his tongue as he went lower.

My sexy ghost monster was going to drive me mad by the time he claimed me.

EIGHT

COLE

SHE'D SAID YES. Joy like I'd never known bubbled inside of me as I kissed my way down my mate's soft skin toward her pussy. I wanted to drown in her taste before I sank my cock inside her. Wrapping a tentacle around each of her legs, I gently spread them wide enough for me to settle between her thighs. Rubbing my nose in the crease next to her entrance, I groaned as her Ghost Orchid scent filled my lungs.

Slipping my palms under her ass, I lifted her until her pussy was right where I wanted it. Her body jerked with a gasp as I took my first deep lick inside her. Fuck, she tasted like heaven. I spent a few minutes slowly tongue fucking her, keeping her arousal on a low boil. When she whimpered, I slipped a tentacle inside, lining up a suction cup with her bundle of nerves as I moved to wrap my lips over her hard, little clit, suckling it. The moment I did, she came with a scream as she shook in my grip.

Removing my tentacle, I covered her core with my mouth, lapping up every bit of cream she gave me. I couldn't get enough. I continued to eat at her until she came again, and only then did I rise up over her, kissing my way back up her luscious body, pausing at her cute, little belly button before moving up to her tits where I nipped, sucked and licked until she was writhing for me once more.

"Cole! I need you inside me."

Moving up, I nipped at her chin before straightening up to look down at her. She was stunning, her beautiful body undulating on the moss bedding, the sunlight coming in through the skylight and windows making her glow. Her cheeks were flushed pink, as was her chest. I'd left several marks over her pale skin that had my cock throbbing as I took in each one. By the time we were done, we'd both have permanent marks on our bodies.

Taking my erection in my hand, I lined it up with her glistening pussy lips, rubbing the head between her folds for a few moments before I looked up to her face to absorb her expression as I slowly pushed in. With a gasp, she arched her back and slapped her palms out against the moss as I bottomed out, tapping her cervix.

"*La sirena*, my mate."

With a smile, she locked her gaze with mine. When she reached her hands up, I leaned forward, wanting her hands on me. A shudder went through me when she gripped my horns and pulled me down to her. I went willingly, pressing my lips to hers and letting her lead the kiss, only breaking it when I started to move, thrusting slowly in and out of her slick heat.

"I love you, Cole. My mate."

"You are my very heart and soul, Katherine."

She clenched down around me, and I couldn't keep going slow, no matter how much I wanted to take my time and savor every moment. With a growl, I started moving faster, holding her hips as I pounded in and out of her willing body. She shifted her hands to my shoulders, gripping me tightly as her breathing grew labored.

Knowing I would be claiming her as my mate had my arousal spiking faster and higher than ever before, and it wasn't long before the telltale tingle ran through me. With one last thrust deep within her, I bared my fangs and bit into her shoulder as I filled her womb with my seed.

Her blood sang across my tastebuds. More potent than her Ghost Orchid scent, it overtook my senses, and I hummed as I swallowed the first mouthful of her lifeforce. When it hit the back of my throat, my dick kicked within her and I came again. Being careful to not seal the wound, I released her, then whispered in her ear, "Your turn, *la sirena.*"

"Wh-what do you mean?"

Her voice was breathy, as though she'd run a marathon.

"You need to bite me hard enough to break the skin and taste me." She stiffened beneath me. "Don't think on it, just do it quickly. Like when I bit you, your bite won't cause me pain."

"But I don't have sharp fangs like you."

I smiled in against her throat, before I moved to lap up the blood trickling down from her wound, careful to not lick over the bite and seal it.

"*La sirena*, bite me now, hard as you can. Let us seal our bond."

My tentacles were surrounding her, making her a nest, and I used them to lift her up until her face was pressed in against the tender flesh at the base of my throat.

With a sigh, she nuzzled her mouth in against me before she took some of my skin between her teeth and bit down.

It took her longer than me to break the surface, but the moment she did, a sensation like I'd never experienced flashed through me, blackening my vision for a few moments as I trembled with intense arousal and love for my mate.

When she released her bite, I lifted away, pulling my cock free from her slick heat. Taking her hand in mine, I guided her down to her pussy, where our cum was mixed together. I made sure both of our palms were coated before I released my grip.

"Press your palm over where you bit me. Our combined cum will seal the wound and our bond."

As I pressed my hand over her shoulder and my mark on her, she did the same. A rush of power flowed through me as we did, strengthening my body and making my cock throb as I came once more, pumping out more cum over my mate's pussy and belly.

As I finished, Katherine cried out before she slipped into unconsciousness in the nest of my tentacles. Panic flared within me for a moment before I remembered Lisa had done the same thing after bonding with Noah. Like my brother's mate had, I was sure Katherine would soon wake.

Keeping her in a comfortable position, I began to use my palms to spread my cum over her skin, making sure I didn't miss an inch from her neck down. I wanted her always covered in my shimmer so no one would ever question that she was claimed and unavailable.

KATHERINE

Every time I thought my orgasms couldn't possibly be more powerful, Cole proved me wrong. The climax that rolled through me after we sealed each other's bite marks left me barely able to breathe. Then a rush of power flowed through my blood, changing me. Pain mixed with pleasure until the world spun before my vision darkened.

My mind came back online to the sensation of Cole's hands running over my body, but I didn't work out what he was doing for a few moments.

"Did you just cover me in shimmer again?"

"I didn't go above your neck, my love. How are you feeling?"

He purred the words while he nibbled along my jaw, distracting me from continuing to tell him off. I mentally made a note to revisit the topic later as I tilted my head to the side, giving him more room as he kissed his way down my throat.

"Good but different."

Unable to keep still, I started stroking my palms over his tentacles, which had made a nest under me as we made love earlier. His skin was slick and so soft and silky, I could touch him all day. Finding a suction cup, I ran my fingertip lightly around it, enjoying how my teasing had his entire body shivering.

When he licked over my shoulder, a jolt of red-hot lust shot through me, having me wrapping my hands around his tentacles and tightening my grip.

"Cole..."

"Yes, my mate? Does that feel good?"

He licked over his bite mark again, and I groaned as a mini orgasm rolled through me.

"So good."

His tentacles shifted a moment before the tip of one began to tease my rear entrance. A shudder ran through me as he began to penetrate me while moving to suck and tease my nipples. Wanting to bring him pleasure, I lifted my hands to his horns, stroking the ribbed lengths in time with the tentacle he was now using to fuck my ass. When his hands slid down to grip my waist, I released his horns and spread my legs wide for him, welcoming the feeling of his thick cockhead pressing against my core before he slid in deep, causing us both to cry out.

The mating had obviously heightened our connection, making every touch and sensation more powerful. Unlike most of our couplings, Cole kept the pace slow, gently making love to me, and I loved every second of it. When our climaxes grew close, he lowered down and pressed his lips over my shoulder. Running my palm up around the back of his neck, I lifted up until I could nuzzle in against my bite mark on him. The moment we both were touching the other's mark, an explosion of arousal shot through me, leaving me gasping as I came hard, clenching down on his thick erection until he jerked within me, filling me with more of his seed.

Once I caught my breath, I stroked my fingers down his cheek.

"Can we go in your pond for a bit?"

He pressed a soft kiss to my lips before he responded, "Of course." Keeping me in my nest of tentacles, he slipped us over the edge of the moss bed and into the water, the cool liquid surrounding us in moments, washing away the sweat and cum from all our couplings.

Closing my eyes with a contented sigh, I enjoyed the water lapping at my skin for a few minutes.

"You'll move in with me now, right?"

Cole's normally confident voice was gone, showing how much he feared my answer.

I rolled toward him, his tentacles falling away as I treaded water while getting in the right position to wrap my arms around his neck. His arms banded around my back, lifting me so I could put my legs around his waist.

"Cole, I didn't agree to mate with you lightly. This is forever for me too. I'll be moving in as soon as I can get all my things here."

He gave me a smirk that had me pausing. "What have you done?"

"I had Henry arrange for some movers to pack up all your things and bring them here. I'm not sure when they'll arrive, but you never need to return to your old apartment."

A shudder ran through me as I

remembered the last time I was in the building.

"That's great. Thank you, babe. I never want to see that place again."

He rubbed his forehead against mine in a sweet touch.

"What about Blackwell Retreat? Do you want to go back to get anything from there? We could send Henry over to grab stuff if you don't. Although, you probably should call William soon."

Pulling back, I looked into his eyes. "What do you mean, I should call? How do you even know who he is?"

"When we came to your apartment looking for you, he was there with a younger man."

My heart sank. "Ash."

Cole nodded, "That was what William called him. It seemed Ash had come for you, and William had followed to stop him."

That had me relaxing. For a moment I'd thought Cole was going to tell me that William had joined with Ash to drag me back home. Releasing my hold on Cole's shoulders, I leaned back, his hands slipping down to my hips. Keeping my legs wrapped tightly around his waist, I moved my hands through the water as I let my upper half float.

"As much as I'd happily never see Ash again, I do need to go back. Not to pack up anything. I brought everything I own with me when I moved out to do the doula course. But I need to explain everything to my mom and William. I was taking the course so I could go back and use what I've learned." Pausing, I waited to be sure I had his full attention. "I still want to do that, Cole. Work as their doula. The women that come to the retreat don't trust easily, especially not outsiders. But I don't need to live there to be able to do that."

Tentacles rose up under my back, supporting me so I could float just under the surface of the water. "So long as you live here and don't mind that I'll always go with you, I'm fine with you going back." He paused a moment. "But know if Ash pulls anything on you, I will defend and protect you."

I smiled up at my gorgeous ghost monster mate, who I knew without a doubt would always keep me safe.

"I'm counting on it, babe. Speaking of your ghostie self...I can see it now, right?"

Within seconds, his body shimmered from his normal blueish purple to a transparent white. While he stayed solid between my legs, I could no longer feel his tentacles beneath me.

"So you can choose what parts of you can be felt?"

His ghostly head nodded. "Yes. In ghost form, I can be fully ghost and move through walls or anything else, or I can make parts of me feel as though I'm in my corporeal form. That's how I fucked you that first time."

Him just saying the word had my body heating up. When I clenched my thighs against his sides on a moan, he tightened his grip on my hips and pulled me down over his erection.

"Hmmm, my ravenous ghost monster."

He growled in response to my husky words.

"For you? Always."

Thank you so much for reading Ravenous Ghost Monster. I hope you enjoyed reading Cole and Katherine's story as much as I did writing it.

If you have a few spare minutes, I'd love it if you could tell others what you thought of Ravenous Ghost Monster by leaving a review online.

If you'd like to know when more Ghost Monster books, or any of my other new releases, will come out, or where you can see me in person, follow the link below to sign up for my newsletter.
newsletter.khloewren.com/ghost2

Keep reading for a teaser from book 1, Insatiable Ghost Monster, Noah and Lisa's story.

Each day I learned something new and fascinating, and I was dreading the day I'd finish with cataloging it all.

That thought had me sitting back in my seat. What was I going to do when this was done? The initial letter only invited me to stay for as long as it took to complete the job. Had that changed now I was Noah's *mascota*, his pet?

Chewing my thumb nail, I pondered that thought. It wasn't like I'd left anything behind to come here, and I really didn't want to leave. Lifting my gaze to the third level, I took in how few rows remained. The job was nearly done. Maybe I should have worked slower, dragged it out so I could stay longer. But would prolonging my departure just make the heartache worse? Would leaving sooner be better?

My vision blurred and I dashed the tears away before they could fall. The last thing I needed was for Noah to see me crying like a baby over something that was a condition from the start. He might kick me to the curb earlier.

"There you are, my little slut."

The voice was like ice down my spine, and I jerked up out of the seat to face the threat before I knew what I was doing.

Christopher's face pulled into an ugly sneer as he stood just inside the doorway.

"Look at you. Naked and ready to go. Fuck, it smells like an orgy in here and I can see the cum on you. You been giving away what isn't yours to sell, babe?"

His to sell? I shook my head as fear and anger mixed together in my belly, causing me to cramp as nausea rose.

"Christopher, I haven't been yours for a long damn time. And I was never yours to sell. That's why I left. What are you even doing here?" *How the hell did you find me this time?*

He prowled toward me slowly as though he knew I had nowhere to go, and he had all the time in the world.

"I'm here to collect what's mine, of course. Nice try hiding out in this old place, but I'll always find you, babe. You're mine.

Always will be. And whoever has been fucking you will pay for the privilege."

My breath stuttered at the reminder I wasn't alone this time. I had a monster to help me. Noah would never allow this bastard to take me. Christopher had no idea the hell that would be unleashed. I wasn't sure where Noah had gone, but clearly it wasn't anywhere nearby, or he'd already be here. I needed to get out of this room and start calling out to him.

My need to get away from Christopher had me ignoring the fact I was buck-ass naked. Christopher had seen it all before, and thanks to Noah carrying me around the mansion naked over his shoulder regularly, I was certain everyone else in the place had seen all of me too.

I stepped to the side as he got closer, skirting around the big table Noah had fucked me on earlier. My heart ached when my gaze caught on the marks we'd left on the shiny surface as I moved around the opposite side to Christopher.

"Looks like you gave the table a workout. Maybe I'll give you a go up there myself. What do you say? Or you want me to bring a few of my buddies over first, give you a train like you love."

Anger built higher as his words had me remembering the torture he'd heaped on me.

"I fucking hated everything you and your sleazy friends did to me, you bastard."

He threw his head back to laugh like he'd already won. I made the most of him being distracted and started to dash for the door. Before I made it more than three steps, he was on me, tackling my body with his and taking us both down to the ground. My glasses went flying but I didn't have time to worry about them.

"Fuck, you're covered in cum, little slut. Normally I don't like sloppy seconds, but you're not giving me a choice. Need to fuck some sense into you. Remind you who you belong to. Because you will be coming home with me today."

Refusing to give in, I wriggled and bucked against his hold. No way would I leave the manor with him. I'd rather die here than be his captive. The sound of his zipper opening had a shiver running down my spine. Him preparing to rape me had panic rising up, which gave me the burst of strength I needed. Focusing my gaze, I planned my attack. Rather than mindless thrashing, I aimed my knee for his now exposed cock and balls. He caught onto my intention and moved, but not fast enough to avoid the blow entirely. The strike was hard enough he rolled away with a curse, and I was on my feet in seconds and out the door, skidding on the polished floor as I sprinted up the hallway.

"Noah! Cole! Henry! Oliver! Anyone! Help me!"

I screamed out the names of everyone I hoped might be in the house. I wished I knew the names of all Noah's siblings. Henry had said three were home, but I only knew Cole's name. Still, surely if they heard me screaming, they'd come, even if they didn't hear their name?

Noah's wing was all the way across the house, but Cole's was just up ahead. I knew I needed to get off this main hallway before Christopher pulled himself together.

"Noah!" I called out before turning down the main hallway of Cole's domain and sprinting again.

"Bitch!"

A shiver ran down my spine at how close Christopher's voice sounded. Feeling exposed in the main hall, I turned into the next room I reached, shoving the door open and rushing inside, barely skidding to a stop before I went face first into a pond.

To read the full story follow the link below:

www.books2read.com/ InsatiableGhostMonster

INSATIABLE GHOST MONSTER

Gallichan Manor Series Book 1

Blurb:

I've been on the run for so long that I've all but forgotten what peace, or the touch of a hot-blooded male, feels like.

Staying one step ahead of my abusive ex has consumed my life for years. So, when a mysterious offer to catalogue a private library in a secluded manor lands on my doorstep, I jump at the opportunity.

But it turns out the manor isn't as empty as I thought. There's at least one ghost monster that roams the halls, but he's not interested in scaring me. No, he's all about awakening my long buried erotic needs and feeding them until I can't think straight.

So caught up in my secluded haven, I forget all about the looming threat hunting me. But this time when my ex finds me, I'm not alone and he's about to get a lethal lesson in how protective an enraged ghost monster can be when his mate is threatened.

'Insatiable Ghost Monster' is the adult Beauty and the Beast re-telling you didn't know you needed. Download your copy today and be swept away by this dark, ghostly romance!

For more details follow this link www.books2read.com/ InsatiableGhostMonster

BIOGRAPHY

Khloe Wren lives in rural South Australia with her husband, two daughters and an ever changing list of animals!

She started writing in 2013 and has published over 50 books since then in the romantic suspense genre. She writes both paranormal and contemporary stories, including her best selling series Charon MC.

Khloe enjoys writing outside of the box and she loves her heroes strong, and her heroines even stronger.

facebook.com/khloe.wren.3

instagram.com/khloewren

bookbub.com/authors/khloewren

www.ingramcontent.com/pod-product-compliance
Lightning Source LLC
Chambersburg PA
CBHW070501170726

48291CB00008B/2608